THE NEW MOON

THE STORY OF DICK MARTIN'S COURAGE,
HIS SILVER SIXPENCE AND HIS FRIENDS
IN THE NEW WORLD

BY
CORNELIA MEIGS

AUTHOR OF "THE WINDY HILL," "THE POOL OF STARS,"
"HELGA AND THE WHITE PEACOCK," ETC.

FRONTISPIECE BY
MARGUERITE DE ANGELI

New York
THE MACMILLAN COMPANY
1925

All rights reserved

COPYRIGHT, 1924,
By THE MACMILLAN COMPANY.

Set up and electrotyped. Published September, 1924. Reprinted December, 1924; July, 1925.

PRINTED IN THE UNITED STATES OF AMERICA BY
THE BERWICK & SMITH CO.

NOTE

The first two chapters of this book were published in the "Youth's Companion" as a short story entitled "Silver Sixpences," and are reprinted by permission.

CONTENTS

CHAPTER		PAGE
I.	Silver Sixpences	1
II.	The New Moon	12
III.	The Man With Rings in His Ears	23
IV.	Cormac	37
V.	Bendemeer's Stream	48
VI.	Burwick Fair	64
VII.	The Shining Road	80
VIII.	Katequa	98
IX.	Wild Honey	120
X.	Companion of the Thunder	134
XI.	The White Prairie	154
XII.	The Shadowy Sioux	174
XIII.	A Bargain in Good Luck	188
XIV.	The Night Watchers	202
XV.	The Eagle Dance	221
XVI.	The Bloom of the Year	232

THE NEW MOON

THE NEW MOON

CHAPTER I

SILVER SIXPENCES

THIS is not a fairy story, although it may set out like one. It has to do with very real things, as you will find out in due time. But it begins on a spring day, with the air so clear, the gold of the sunshine so bright, and the birds' voices so loud that it seemed to be a time when fairy tales might begin to come true; or when real things were so strangely beautiful that they might reach out, at any moment, and touch the glittering edge of magic. Young Dick Martin, as he sat on the doorstep of his tumbledown cottage, basking in the first warm sunshine of spring, was thinking vaguely of just such matters. His head was very full of fairy stories, told to him in the long winter evenings by Bridget Anne; and his heart was full of a tingling interest in all the strange adventures that are really possible in the future of a half grown boy. Yet his ideas could not have been put into words; if he had been asked what he was thinking, he would have had to answer, "Nothing."

A few tufts of green grass were sprouting at the edge of the crooked doorstone; and the climbing rose that grew up to the eaves of the battered thatched roof was beginning to unfold tiny red leaves. There was nothing old or shabby about the shining green of the grass-blades or the crinkled freshness of the new leaves on the rose vine; but everything else about the place was as battered and worn out as it well could be, and still hold together. From the holes in the thatch, to the patches of mud on Dick's ragged trousers, there was nothing that did not want rebuilding or repairing or doing away with entirely.

Yet Dick's round face showed a smile of pleasant content, as he stretched his legs to the sun and thrust his hands deep into his pockets, that had holes in them. Inside the half open door he could hear the sound of a broom sweeping vigorously, and of a voice singing; while a yellow-billed blackbird, lifting his voice in rivalry from the blossoming hedge, was whistling the gayest bird song in all of Ireland. Very gradually his thoughts came back to the homely things about him.

"If we had a garden, now, it would be all growing up in roses and lilies and cabbages for the big pot," he was reflecting. "I do wonder, sometimes, why our garden doesn't grow like other people's."

The last was really a thought for himself, but he spoke it out loud, for the door had opened wide behind him, and the broom was sweeping the dust from the earth floor out upon the doorstep.

"What is it you were saying?" said Bridget Anne, leaning upon her broom handle. "Did you wonder why this garden doesn't grow? Ah, it used to be a beautiful bit of ground once, I'm told. Did you never know that in your great-great-grandfather's day there used to be a spell on it?"

"I've heard people say such a thing, but I never knew just the right of it," answered Dick.

"You were likely too little for your mother to tell you, and I don't know just the story, myself," said Bridget Anne. "Some day you had better ask the little old woman at the edge of the wood, *she* knows everything."

"I will," returned Dick slowly. The blackbird in the hedge, at the sound of their voices, had fluttered away in frightened haste, so that Dick, perhaps, seeing the great show of busy wings, felt ashamed to be so lazy on such a fine spring morning.

"I will go now," he said, and marched down the flagstones to the gate that stood partly open because it had only one hinge and would not shut.

The little village where Dick Martin lived was

in another land from this, and was so far away from everywhere that some of the country folk told one another it stood at the very end of the world. People who knew more, and who had looked into geography books said it was not at the end of the world, since it was in Ireland; but that it was the most beautiful place in the world—that every one must know. The people in the one crooked street chatted with one another in Gaelic, the ancient Irish tongue, and had changed scarcely any of the ways that their fathers used a hundred years ago. Dick knew some English, but, so far, had had little need to use it.

Beyond the handful of thatched houses lay a strip of open fields, where the brown grass was turning green in the hollows. Beyond the fields, in turn, was a stretch of woods, where the trees were just showing the thin mist of little leaves at the tips of the branches. Although he could not see it, Dick well knew that the wood ended at the edge of a high cliff, and below it lay a stretch of white sand, where the great, restless sea came tumbling in with waves that were never weary, and a voice that was never still. The boy used to love to lie at the top of the cliff and watch the changing water below and the far, blue horizon where ships passed. To him it always seemed, not the end, but the beginning of the world.

He was neither a very little boy, nor a very big one, but the size just between; yet for all that, he was oversmall to be all alone in the world. He had no father or mother; all he had was the cottage and the bit of ground around it, for they both belonged to him. Bridget Anne and her husband, Michael More, a young couple quite as poor as himself, lived in the cottage and had Dick live with them in the place of paying rent to him. There was never much to eat on the bare board table, but there was always laughter around it, for the three were all young and light-hearted and fond of one another. Michael worked at one of the farms beyond the village and was always up and off by daylight, whistling gayly as he went trudging away to his heavy labor. They all lived nearly a hundred years ago, so that Bridget Anne still put out a bowl of milk for the fairies every night, and always found it empty in the morning. She had learned from her mother, and she from her mother before her, where to look for leprecauns— though she had never found one—how to tell fortunes in the chimney smoke, and what day was the luckiest in the year to begin a journey. People shook their heads often and said that times had changed, and that it was many a long year now since any one had really seen the Little People, but that you could never be sure they were clean gone away for good.

Dick, as he walked along, was much tempted to leave the highroad and take the twisting path that led away across the field and through the wood to the cliff above the sea. He was just at the age when it is easy to forget one errand by thinking of another; but this time, perhaps on account of seeing the yellow-billed blackbird again, pecking at the roadside, he remembered where he was going. He wondered now how it had happened that he could have heard scraps of that tale of his great-great-grandfather and one of the Little People and not have tried, long before, to find out the whole truth of the matter.

The cottage to which he came was even smaller than his own; but it was very spruce and neat, with its whitewashed walls and tidy thatch and bright-colored crocuses and daffodils coming into bloom in the dooryard. For many years the little old woman had earned her bread by spinning. So many people had brought her their wool and flax and had stayed to tell her all their troubles and perplexities and to receive her encouraging advice, that it had come to seem as though she really knew everything about the lives around her. One might almost think it was hopes and happy fancies and dreams of pleasant things that she was spinning for them, instead of linen or woolen thread. People would come to ask her everything, from what to do about a lost sweetheart to where to look for a strayed puppy.

Like every one else, she was welcoming the new

spring sunshine by sitting before her door among the daffodils. Her spinning wheel was beside her, and it was whirring away while she smiled to herself as though it was some particularly happy dream she was putting into the bride's linen upon which she was at work.

She stopped, however, to greet Dick and to listen to his questions.

"Yes," she said, "I have heard about that matter. Wind up this reel of thread for me, there's a good boy, while I tell you what I know."

When she had set the humming wheel in motion again, she began:

"Your great-great-grandfather had a garden and what was more, he owned the ground himself. That's a rare thing nowadays and it was rarer then; but by his thrift he had saved up, little by little, to make it his own. He had a kind landlord who was willing to see him have his wish as perhaps another would not have done. The very day that the cottage and land were made over to him, there happened that strange thing that left the place lucky for all time. But it is such an old story that what truth there ever was in it has long been forgotten, so that whatever people tell now seems but a fairy tale."

"But just what was it that happened?" Dick demanded.

"I don't say that I know just what happened, but

this is what people say. On the day I speak of, a little man in a ragged, green cloak came in through the gate and asked the new owner and his young wife for food. It was only a cup of thin porridge and the heel of a loaf of bread that were given him, for it was all that the two had in the house. But the little fellow was grateful, and he promised that every season when the garden was dug, there should be a silver sixpence found at the end of every row. It was so, all through your great-great-grandfather's life, a shining, silver sixpence at the end of every row he might dig. But when he died the charm ended, and no such thing happens now."

"Now what I want to know," said Dick, busy with the thread, of which he had tangled more than he had wound, "what I want to know is how can a body bring such good luck back again?"

"And where is the garden?" inquired the old woman. "Your great-great-grandfather did not carry it away with him."

"No, we have the bit of land still, but the ground is trodden as hard as iron and all grown up with thorns and briars."

"And your house is a tumbledown place with sagging thatch and straw stuffed into the windows, now isn't it?" went on the woman. "It was so even in your father's time, and all the while your father and your father's father never thought of digging in the garden."

"Maybe they tried it once and found nothing," Dick answered. "They hadn't the promise of the little green man."

"And what's to hinder some one from working in it now?" she inquired. "You think Michael More is too busy with his farm work, but how about you, a great boy with legs growing out of his breeches and arms coming out of his sleeves, as yours are? You're big enough to tend a garden. As for the promise of the little green man, I'll give you a like one. Go home and dig up that same garden, plant it and till it, and you will find a sixpence for every row, only mind you, dig deep."

Dick thanked her for her promise, although in his heart he was doubtful of its power. He finished his task of reeling the thread, which, on account of his awkwardness with the tangles, took him a long time. Then he stood up to go. "Would it be a lucky day to begin now?" he asked.

"To-day is always a luckier day than to-morrow," she replied, "and I think that a boy who would get my thread into such a tangle and then get it out again is the kind of boy who has good luck. It may be, too, that you have an eye for magic things, seeing that one of your forbears was spoken to by one of the Little People. Such things, they say, live on in families."

Dick said good-by and trudged home through the gay, green world. Once more the little path across the field to the sea seemed to beckon to him, but he passed it by. He reached home quickly and turned at once from the rickety gate to the weed-filled garden. Usually when he went there, it was to sit under the thorn hedge and watch the big, white clouds sailing overhead, but now that pastime must come to an end. Dick got to work.

Day after day he labored to cut down the weeds, to grub up the brambles, and make the garden fit for proper things once more. It was a long task and a toilsome one, for the hard soil had not been disturbed for years; and, in spite of what the old woman had said, Dick was not such a very big boy, after all. The thorns scratched him and made his tattered clothes more ragged than ever; the spade and the hoe blistered his hands; but he worked on. He was no longer sure that he believed the promise of the old woman; perhaps he was not even certain of the truth of that tale about his great-great-grandfather and the little green man. But he was bound to finish what he had once begun.

It was May when he finally had the garden clear, and a warm May night with the moon just rising when he was ready to dig the first row. The moist, black earth smelt sweet as it crumbled under his spade, and as he dug and dug until he came to the end.

"There is nothing there," he was just saying to himself, when "clink" there came the sound of metal against his blade. He saw something on the ground that winked and glittered in the moonlight.

He picked it up quickly, thinking only that here, after all, was proof that there was truth in that story out of the distant past. He had little thought of the future, and of the strange and far adventures on which he and that silver sixpence were to go together.

CHAPTER II

THE NEW MOON

DICK straightened his back and began to rub, against his sleeve, the coin that he had found. It was bigger and thinner than the pieces of money he knew, but it certainly was a silver sixpence.

"So it was a true charm after all!" he cried as he picked up his spade and began to dig at the next row with all the energy that was in him.

He worked so late that the moon failed him; he got up early the next morning and toiled all day until every row was dug, but he found nothing more.

"Maybe they will work to the top when I do the hoeing," he tried to hope, and so he planted the rows and tilled them, day by day. The pale green leaves of cabbages came up, the thick blades of turnips, and the brittle stalks of potatoes. Never a weed dared show its head above the earth, for he was always going up and down the rows with his hoe, still thinking that some day he would once more hear that clink against the blade and would see the silver gleaming from the black earth. But never a sixpence did he find. Yet the old woman had said that the charm was still there and that he was a boy with an eye for fairy things!

Many a time he was tempted to throw away his hoe and sit down under the hedge to take his ease and watch the clouds sail across the sky; but he was beginning to be fond of his green things that were standing so neat and trim where once had been only weeds and briars. He had not the heart to let them die.

"But the old woman promised me falsely," he kept grumbling to himself, "and some day I will go back to her house and tell her so. But I have no time now, with the weeds growing up so fast."

He worked all through the summer, and had potatoes and onions and many a good thing besides for Bridget Anne to put into the pot. Moreover, when autumn came, he had a great barrowload of vegetables and sweet, dried herbs to carry to market. He took them to the fair one bright fall day and sold everything he had within an hour.

Bridget Anne had sewed up the holes in his pockets in preparation for the money he was to get. He had saved three heads of cabbage and a handful of herbs to carry to the cottage of the old woman, for he felt grateful to her in his heart, even though she had promised him what was not true.

She was sitting by the door, spinning in the autumn sunshine, just as she had sat there in the pleasant warmth of spring. Very gravely she listened to what he had to tell, and she nodded wisely when he drew out the thin, old silver sixpence that he had found.

"But there's money jingling in your pocket still," she declared. "How did that come there, if you found nothing?"

"Oh, that is for what I sold at the market," he told her.

"How many rows did you have in your garden?" she asked, and—

"Twenty-five," he answered her. "I have counted them a hundred times."

"Now that money that you have, if it were all in sixpences, how many would it make?" she asked him again, and he counted slowly, for that was a hard sum to do in his head. He went to school, part of the year, to the village priest; but there were some things he had not yet learned.

"Twenty-five," he cried at last. "Glory me, there's a sixpence for every row!"

The old woman said never a word, but sat twirling her wheel and smiling to herself.

"But how about the one sixpence I found?" he asked. "If that was not magic, how did it come there?"

"Your great-great-grandfather must have left it," she said, "just to hold the luck until some one like

THE NEW MOON 15

himself should come to till the garden again. He was a wise man, and had the eye for fairy things, as you have, too. Others who came after him were content to sit under the thorn bush and watch the clouds go by, but if you keep on as you have begun, the garden should yield silver sixpences to the end of time."

Dick walked home through the hazy autumn twilight, turning the money in his pocket and thinking of many happy things. His own little cottage, with the smoke rising from the crooked chimney, and with the red light shining behind the windows, looked sweeter to him than it had ever looked before.

"I'll spend some of this money to have the thatch mended," he thought, "so that the rain and snow won't drip on our beds when the winter comes, and I will buy Bridget Anne a new rosary, for her old one is mended in four places."

All through the cold months he was thinking of what he would do with the garden the next year and even the year after that. The snow was scarcely off the ground in the spring before he was at his digging again. No sitting on the sunny doorstone for him! Things had changed for Dick Martin.

Things were to change still more, in the strange way they have of turning suddenly upside down about a person's ears, all in a day or night. Although his own piece of ground had done well in the past year, it was, so it seemed, the only bit of Ireland that had prospered. The crops had been scanty everywhere and, though things were not so bad as in some of the terrible famine years, there was bitter poverty in the village that winter, and in Dick Martin's house. Bridget Anne had often shed tears over the thin porridge and the bread that was coarser and blacker than ever.

"It will be better in the spring," she kept telling Dick and Michael; but spring seemed long in coming.

The boy was too young to understand how badly things were going, and what the results were to be for himself. He had heard older people complain of hard times before and thought that they always did so. He was, therefore, not in the least prepared for what was to come.

He saw Michael More come home early one afternoon but thought little of it. Later, however, when he came to the end of his own task and went toward the house with a great and comfortable happiness within him for the good day's work he had done, and a great hunger for the supper that was simmering in the pot, Bridget Anne met him at the door.

"Oh, Dick, here's news," she cried, and he sat down on the threshold to hear it, feeling a sudden, queer coldness inside him where the warm happiness had been.

"There's no more work for Michael at the Driscoll's farm because of the hard times. But he's been promised a place at the great farm over Casterbrook way, if I will go, too, for work in the kitchen. And we must go to-morrow if we are to have the chance at all. It breaks my heart to be leaving you, Dick: we've been so happy in this cottage, even if this last winter we've been hungry in it, too."

Dick was silent, not knowing what to say, nor indeed just what this change would mean to him. Would he have to live alone in the cottage? He might be able to manage by himself, he thought, for he was a big boy now, up to Bridget Anne's shoulder, although it was true that beside that long giant, Michael More, he seemed still very little.

"You will get other tenants as good as we," faltered Bridget Anne. "Michael spoke to Tom Reilly and his wife as he came home, and they half promised to come. Otherwise we could never bear to leave you alone."

Michael More said as little as did Dick concerning the change, but each understood the other without words. Bridget Anne, talking and working continuously, and weeping as she toiled, was busy half the night with her preparations. But she found, somehow, an hour to sit down and tell him one last story, such as she had so often told as they all sat together by the fire. It was not of fairies and good luck charms this time, but of saints and miracles and of the seven archangels who fly above the heavens with shining wings and faces like white flame.

"And may they watch over us," she ended, wiping her eyes, "and bring us to dwell together once again."

She and Michael set off in the morning, each with a bundle, while Dick stood at the gate, watching them go with a heavy heart.

"It may be the change will be a great thing for all of us," Bridget Anne had said at the last, "for it has come just at the time of the new moon and that always brings good fortune. If Tom Reilly fails you, go to the little spinning woman; she will tell you what to do. I have set the pot on the fire, so there will be your dinner ready to-day, at least. Don't watch us out of sight, Dick darling, for that will be bad luck. Make a wish on the new moon to-night, and Michael and I will do the same, and maybe it will bring great fortune for us all."

Dick was careful not to watch them out of sight; but went to dig busily in his garden for the whole of the morning. When the sun stood high at noontime, he went in to eat his dinner.

It was strange to eat it alone at the rough table where he had had company for so long. Before he had finished his meal he found himself clattering loudly with the dishes, to break the deathly silence that filled the cottage. He listened to the branches

THE NEW MOON 19

of the rose vine fretting against the window frame, and to the faint sound of the fire flickering on the hearth, and in sudden panic he put down, untasted, his last spoonful of soup. He was afraid to hear himself swallow!

He went to seek Tom Reilly, but found only his wife at home. Perhaps the good-natured Tom might have been kinder, but sharp-tongued Peggy wasted few words in telling him what she thought of the plan.

"We do better here, so why should we move into another cottage, and have another mouth to feed? It would be only charity to do it, and this is a hard year for charity. So go on to somebody else, you with your house and land of your own, and you hardly taller than my elbow!"

So few people that she knew owned their own small cottages and patches of garden, that she was probably jealous that a boy so young should be a landowner. But what she said of charity stung him, so that he had no heart to look farther for a tenant for his tumbledown cottage.

"I will ask the little old woman who spins," he decided.

When he came to her house, however, he saw that the door was closed and the shutters barred, with last autumn's dead leaves drifted under the windows. It was plain that the winter had been such a hard one that she had gone to stay with one of her children or grandchildren until times should be better. Standing on her doorstone before the empty cottage, Dick knew for the first time what it was to feel absolutely alone in the world.

He walked away down the road, thinking of his own little house and how blank the windows would look and how dead and cold the hearth would be where Bridget Anne always had kept her cheerful fire. It was the end of the day now, shadows were growing long, and the house would be full of twilight, with a feeling of creepy things in the corners. He felt that he could not go back to it just yet. Without thinking much of where he was going he took the crooked path that led across the field and into the wood. It was shadowy among the tall trees: but outdoors is never so fearsome at twilight as an empty and lonely house. The spring wind was talking in the treetops, where the buds were growing big and showed fat or feathery against the pink sky. He had only a little way to go before he came out upon the cliff above the sea.

The waves were talking also on the beach below, with voices that sounded friendly as they washed up upon the soft sand. He lay down upon the short grass and watched them as they came splashing in and went sliding out, one after another. There came around the point a tall, beautiful ship, with three masts, and every one of her square white sails set to the evening breeze. She was like a great cloud of white, touched with rose and gold, and moved along as easily as if she were indeed a cloud sailing above the sunset. His heart gave a sudden jog inside him, as it always did when he saw such a ship.

"She is going to the Americas," he thought. "What—what if I should be going with her!"

He lay down on the new grass, which was still dry and warm from the hot spring sunshine, and watched her out of sight. When a second point of land had at last hidden her, he got up with a great sigh. It was growing quite dark now and he must go home.

Suddenly he remembered what Bridget Anne had said of the new moon. He must make a wish on it, being careful to look at it first over his right shoulder, while he turned over the money in his pocket. There was nothing there but the sixpence he had found in the garden, for he had spent all the rest long ago and had only kept his grandfather's coin as a luck piece. He stood up, with his back to the fading sunset, and craned his head over his right shoulder. There was the tiny new moon showing in the fading sky, a thread of silver at the edge of the old moon's shadowy globe.

"I wish good fortune to Bridget Anne and to

Michael More; and that I should know what to do," he said aloud.

He moved back to get a better view of the moon over his shoulder; stepped beyond the edge of the cliff; and went over backward into space.

CHAPTER III

THE MAN WITH RINGS IN HIS EARS

THE cliff was not at its highest where Dick fell, moreover the sand was soft below, and he himself was light, and with muscles, each as hard as a twisted juniper branch. He was, therefore, not much hurt beyond some bruises and a singing in his head. After a moment he sat up and looked dizzily about him.

There was a man standing before him, a square-shouldered, dark-faced fellow with a red handkerchief tied over his head and with gold hoops in his ears. In contrast to his sunburned face, his teeth gleamed very white when he smiled. It was a friendly smile, that lit up his dark features and made Dick feel that though the stranger looked like a pirate, he was nothing more strange than a sailor from beyond the seas.

"Are you hurt?" he asked anxiously, and then as Dick, struck by a sudden thought, began feeling about him in the sand—"Have you lost anything?" he questioned further.

"My sixpence," Dick said. "I was turning it over

in my pocket to wish on the new moon and it must have fallen out when I was upside down in the air."

"I was making a wish myself," returned the other, "and here you came tumbling down upon me as though you had fallen out of that very moon. You might be the answer to my wish, though I can say you hardly look like it."

Although he was so brown that he might have been a Portuguese or even a Malay, he spoke the Gaelic tongue, so that it was evidently only sunburn that disguised this Irish seafaring man. His eyes were dark blue like Dick's own, and they were as kind and friendly as his smile.

"It is getting too dark to see anything clearly. Shall we light a bit of driftwood to find the sixpence that fell out of you?" he suggested.

He struck a spark with the flint and steel from his pocket, caught it on some dry seaweed and presently had a little blaze.

"If you do not find it, I can give you another," he said, "for sailors do not come home empty-handed, and I have been only an hour ashore. It is strange that wishing on the new moon should rob you even of what you had."

Dick thanked him, but tried to explain that it was this one sixpence, and not any other, that he so greatly desired. He gathered a further handful of the smooth waterworn chips that strewed the

THE MAN WITH RINGS IN HIS EARS 25

shore; and built up the fire to such leaping ruddy flames that a moment later the sailor's quick eye singled out a flash of silver in the sand.

"Here it is," he exclaimed. "Yes, I see it is not quite like other sixpences. Now tell me how you came to get it."

He sat down on a stone beside the fire, drew out a black and very bad-smelling pipe and lighted it at the blaze. Dick sat in the warm sand beside him and told him of the garden and the little old woman, of his great-great-grandfather and the small, green man. Led on by the man's interested questioning, the boy, in the end, told him everything, of the departure of Bridget and Michael, of Peggy Reilly's sharp words, and of the lonely cottage that was his only home.

"What is a boy to do that has no kin or friends in all of Ireland?" he asked at the end of his tale.

"Have you ever thought," said the other slowly, "of sailing away to the Americas? There is a fair green country, so people tell to me who have seen only the edge of it; and it has room, as it seems, for every one. I have seen the rocks and the headlands and pine woods of its north coast; I have put in at the wide sandy, green harbors to the south; and I have seen the forest of masts and the slow blue water of that hot port on the gulf that is at the mouth of the great Mississippi. It looks everywhere like a friendly land. Would you think of going, lad?"

Dick gasped. What thoughts he had often had when ships went by of sailing off with them! But such dreams had always seemed as remote as those of going to heaven some day.

"How could I get there?" he inquired blankly.

"There's ships with great sails will take you there gladly enough, if you have the passage money," the sailor assured him easily. A man who has wandered over the wet parts of the earth for years and a boy who has never left his own village do not look at such a voyage in the same light. "And while we have been talking," the man went on, "I have been thinking this. Every lad who stops ashore thinks of traveling to far countries some day; and just as truly does every wandering sailor dream of coming home to abide in peace on a little land that he can call his own and where he need not take orders from any man. I am not so young as once I was, and I was sick with yellow fever this last voyage, so I have thought that this was the time for me to go after my dream and make it true. If I were a different sort of a man I would ask you to dwell here with me, but"—he dropped his voice a little—"I am not just fit for a boy to live with, after roaming the world as I have. That cottage and garden of yours seem like what I have been

THE MAN WITH RINGS IN HIS EARS

looking for, since I do not want to take words from a landlord, having taken too many from ships' masters." He knocked out his pipe against the stone upon which he sat and turned to look down keenly at the boy in the firelight.

"I do not ask you to sell me the ground forever, but suppose I give you a gold pound for every sixpence you got out of the garden last year, and in return you are to let me have the land for my use just as I like, as long as I live? When you will be coming home a rich man from the Americas, I will be old enough to want no more ground than a man needs to sleep in to Judgment Day. What do you say? Is it a bargain?"

Dick did not answer the last question at once.

"You have really seen the Americas, both of them? And you want to come back to this village?"

"I've seen all three of them," the sailor responded, "North and South, and the little one in the middle where there is more adventure to a mile of shore line than in both of the others. I brought away from that one a bucketful of silver Spanish dollars, which I lost in a month, and this scar across my hand which I will not lose in a lifetime. But you are not looking for such adventures as mine, you are looking for a new home, since the old one is bare and empty. Will you go?"

Dick sat thinking. It had grown quite dark now, while the tide had crept away, leaving a stretch of sand so wet that the red of the fire was reflected in it. The breeze had dropped and the whisper of the waves was very low. Dick's voice was lower still as he put one more question.

"Could—could I get all the way to the Americas—alone?"

"We needn't think of your trying such a hard thing as that," was the reply. "There's a man I saw at the near-by port that plans to take a flock of sheep over in the next ship, and he said to me did I know a likely lad that was going that way and could lend him a hand. Thomas Garrity his name is. He would watch over you a bit and maybe pay part of your passage for what help you could give him. He'd be a staunch friend to you when you got across, and put you in the way of making a living. There's not much room in this crowded Ireland, for a boy who has no kin. It was through knowing that, I went to sea myself."

Dick was quiet while three waves came in.

"I'd like to do it," he declared.

"I knew you were the man for it," cried the sailor; "and now that's settled, suppose we have a bite of supper."

He pulled out a package of slices of bread and cheese, which they toasted before the fire and then

THE MAN WITH RINGS IN HIS EARS 29

devoured hungrily. Although the food tasted of tar and Virginia tobacco and of other things that might chance to be a sailor's pockets, it was very good.

"I was going to your village, for it is the town where I was born," he explained as they were eating, "and I remembered the shortest way was along the shore. It was because I saw you in the twilight, standing against the sky, and because I saw you weren't watching your feet and might fall over, that I happened to be waiting below. But it has been a good thing for both of us that we wished on the new moon."

When he had finished eating and had brushed away the crumbs in the tidy way that sailors have, he smoked another pipe out almost in silence. Dick wondered whether they ought not to go, but the man at last directed him to put more wood on the fire and sit down again beside him. The red light glowed on his face, making it like some dark picture, with his bright eyes, his thin cheeks, and his wide smile. He leaned forward with his hands on his knees, and was quiet for a moment more, although it was plain that he had something further to say.

"There is a thing you must remember, when you are setting out for strange places, and that is that always—wherever you go—you must take your courage with you. There will be times when things seem so hard that if you turn one way, it's bad, and if you turn another, it's worse, and there's but one thing to do—to go forward. It's often a terrible lot of trouble to be brave, but you must be it when there's naught else to do."

Dick nodded. "I'll try to," he agreed, "but it—it's not always easy." He thought of the empty cottage where he must go back, alone, in the dark, and he could not forbear shivering a little.

"Wherever you go, hold up your head and that will hold up your heart. A rich man takes much money on a journey, but a poor man goes as well laden if he only takes his courage with him."

"I'll remember it," Dick said. "If I have to be brave, why, somehow, I will."

"I will tell you a tale," said the sailor, "a very short tale it is, but worth remembering. Long, long ago when there were many kings in Ireland and as many more in Scotland, there was a king of one country had a great quarrel with a king in the other. They sent word to each other back and forth by carrier pigeons and by the masters of ships, and every word was a bitter and a boasting one.

" 'My kingdom has the most people,' says the king in Scotland.

" 'My people have the bravest hearts,' says the king in Ireland.

" 'My country has the highest mountains,' says the king in Scotland.

" 'And mine has the highest men,' says the king in Ireland.

"And to prove that saying, he sends over to Scotland the great Irish giant, Finn McCoul, who was higher than any man you could dream about. It took the biggest and the bravest ship to carry him, and they had a heavy voyage of it before he came ashore at his journey's end.

"The king in Scotland had no man so tall and he put great tasks on the Irish giant to try his strength. But in the end he spoke scornful and ungrateful words to Finn McCoul, for he said, 'What use is it to be so big, except to eat up the living of ten men in a year?'

" 'There's great use in it,' says the Irish giant, 'for I can do many things that ten men cannot.'

" 'Then prove it, by going home to your own country quicker than it took a ship with ten oarsmen on a side to bring you here,' says the king in Scotland.

" 'That I will,' says the Irish giant, and he strides down to the shore of the sea and it's only when he gets there that he remembers that he cannot swim. But the Scotch king and his men were mocking behind him, so he stepped out bravely from the shore where the surf was rolling in. At the first step the water came up to his knees and at the second it came up to his middle. At the third it was up to his neck, and the waves came lapping against his chin. One more stride and it seemed sure they would go over his head, and for the one time in all his life, Finn McCoul was afraid. He could not go back, with the Scotch king there to jeer at him, and he could not go to one side nor the other. He looked before him and there was the sweet, green coast of Ireland, and the white waves on the rocks, and the hills blue beyond the fields. And he shuts his eyes and takes one more giant step—and the water is rippling round his knees, and out he comes, dripping and splashing, on the shore of his own land."

"But he was a giant," faltered Rick, "and I———"

"Sure, you're a boy going to be a man sometime, and as well able to go forward as a giant. So that's all I have to tell, and now you must be getting home."

"Will you come to sleep at my—at your—at our house?" asked Dick as he got up.

"I must lodge with some friends in the village," the other answered, "and if you are to be a man of the world, it would be good to begin by sleeping in that empty house by yourself. If you can not only go in, but sleep sound until morning, then I will know you are the boy I take you for."

Half an hour later, Dick came up to the door of his house, alone. What dark shadows there were

THE MAN WITH RINGS IN HIS EARS 33

under the eaves, and how black it looked inside the windows! The little moon had long since set, so that only the light of the stars served him as he stumbled over the doorstone and fumbled for the latch. If only there had been one red, winking coal on the hearth to welcome him, it would not have been so hard; but the fire had quite gone out, and the ashes were cold. While he kindled a new fire and watched the flame struggle for life and threaten every moment to die away again, he felt that a thousand terrible things were hidden in the corner of the room and would presently march out upon him. He forced himself to turn and look steadily over his shoulder.

"There is nothing there," he said firmly, and with his words felt his fears vanish. A moment later the fire had caught.

So long he sat on the settle by the hearth, thinking over all that had happened, that in the end he fell asleep with his head against his arm. Two hours later he awoke, roused by a sound at the door. He listened and was about to drop asleep again when he heard it once more, not a knock or a footstep, only a soft movement at the threshold.

He looked out of the window and saw that the stars had been hidden by a rush of clouds. He could hear the wind rising and the patter of rain on the roof. Perhaps it was the wind, perhaps it was a push from outside that loosened the latch and let the door swing slowly open.

He tried to ask, "Who is it?" but his voice refused to make a sound.

The firelight shone out into the dark and lit the drops of water dripping from the thatch, and showed also a small, wet form crawling across the threshold. The midnight visitor was no wayfarer, nor any darkness-haunting goblin, it was a shaggy and dripping puppy, which came slipping past him into the room to throw himself down with a weary sigh before the fire. As Dick stooped down to speak to him, he dropped his pricked ears and feebly wagged a bedraggled tail.

Probably he had thrust his pointed nose against every threshold in the village, and had felt the loneliness at the door of this single one where he had stopped to scratch. Boy and dog slept nestled together for the rest of the night, and Dick's slumbers were sound, even dreamless. He awoke early to see a rain-drenched, sunny world, and to hear a blackbird once more singing in the hedge.

The business of transferring Dick's property to the sailor's keeping and the sailor's money to Dick's pocket was quickly attended to in the presence of the village notary. Dick had scarcely ever seen a gold sovereign before, and could hardly believe that all these could be his, that were piled upon the table.

THE MAN WITH RINGS IN HIS EARS

He brought out his lucky piece to see how it would look beside them. The sailor took it up to examine it once more by daylight.

"It was a good promise the green elf made to your great-great-grandfather, and one or the other of them was a wise man. It's sixpences that are the coin of life, not sovereigns nor gold doubloons nor Spanish pieces-of-eight, but jingling, silver sixpences. It's the little coins and the little minutes that make a life happy in the end. You'll have, as you go forward, some exciting days, some great hours that you will long look back upon; but what you will love to remember will be the small things, the silver, shining minutes like little silver sixpences, that will make up your life's fortune."

"I will thank you always for your plan and the good bargain you have made for me," said Dick, trying his best to voice his gratitude to the true friend he had found in his loneliness.

"You will thank me more, some day, for the advice I've given you," replied the other. "You'll carry out the plan and spend the money got by the bargain; but I hope you will remember always what I have said to you. With the silver sixpence in your pocket, and with a store of real courage in your heart, you are safe to go to the world's end."

It was at sunrise, some days after the new moon, that Dick set out upon his journey to the seaport.

He had spent some of his money to buy new boots and some whole, stout clothes; so that he looked like a different boy from the ragged one who had toiled in the garden. On his shoulder was a bundle holding all his property, and at his heels followed the shaggy collie dog. All search for a possible owner had, so far, brought no result, nor would the puppy look at any one but his newly chosen master. The sailor had offered him a home, but this the dog had plainly declined. It was quite evident that he, too, had a desire to see America.

CHAPTER IV

CORMAC

THE boy's shadow and the dog's, long-legged and ridiculous, stretched down the road before them as they tramped along in the freshness of the early morning. The hedges were in bloom, sending forth waves of sweetness as the white, laden branches swung in the soft wind. The blackbird that had sung so often in his own hedge flew along from branch to branch, opening his orange bill and swelling his glossy throat in a burst of rippling music. It was as though he were trying to say, "Listen to me, you will hear nothing like this where you are going."

The puppy frisked and barked at him, driving him from one perch to another, until he balanced, finally, upon the topmost branch of a thorn bush in the hedge, and sang them out of sight.

No, Dick was thinking, he would hear nothing like that where he was going, he would see nothing like the little square fields or the stony lanes or the thatched cottages, small and cozy and familiar, that stood inside the sagging gates. What would he hear and see instead? The future was like the blank, white page of a book, since he had not the least or vaguest knowledge as to what sort of a place America was. It might contain dragons and fiery serpents and horses with wings for all he knew.

He fell to wondering, also, about Thomas Garrity, who was to be his companion on the journey and his comrade for who knew how long after. If he was like the sailor he would be open-hearted and kindly and full of talk, a person with whom it would be easy to pass the long hours of the voyage.

"I have sent him word he is to meet you at the dock, the morning the ship sails," the sailor had said.

"How am I to know him?" Dick had asked.

"You will not fail to know him in a minute," was the answer. "Just pick out the man who looks entirely unlike all those about him, and that will be Thomas Garrity. He may be a little stiff in his manners at first; but you will find in time that he is a different man inside."

"But what is he like?" persisted Dick.

"It is hard for a man to tell much about any one who is such a friend as Thomas Garrity is to me. When he was young he had the gayest spirit in all of Ireland and a voice, when he sang, that would melt the heart within you. But trouble came on him. When he was working over in another county, his landlord turned his old mother and father out of their cottage, and his mother died of it, they say. It was one of those hard years when few could afford to have pity. Thomas Garrity went away to America and prospered; for he was able to send back money for his father's support and comfort until the old man died. But he himself was a changed man from the day he came home and found the cottage empty and his mother dead. People never heard him sing again."

"Is he big?" Dick was still wondering how he was to know him when they met.

"Yes, he's big, with great, broad shoulders that begin to stoop a little. His hair is going gray, too. But never you worry about how he looks. Don't I tell you that you will know him because he is different from other men? And then there will be the sheep. There will be no other putting sheep aboard a ship to sail for America."

The sun was high and hot, and the dust was deep in the road, when Dick stopped under a great, round, oak tree to eat his lunch and drink from the spring under the hedge. The dog sat with his nose against his new master's knee, eying every bite he ate, and hastily swallowing his own share as it was handed him, bit by bit.

Afterward Dick lay on his back under the tree for a pleasant, lazy hour, watching the sun come shining down between the thick, dark green leaves. He felt that he must look at everything more closely than he had ever looked before, so that he might carry away a more vivid memory of all these things he was not to see again. A little brown hare peeping timidly between two bushes, a red-spotted beetle climbing a long blade of grass at his elbow, a tiny gray bird that crept along the rough bark of the tree above him—all these seemed to him the most beautiful things in the world. Presently, however, the dog nudged him with his long nose, sneezed in the dust, and wagged his tail invitingly, bidding him be upon his way again.

As he sat up the dog came close, and resting his head upon Dick's arm, looked long and steadily up into his face. They had been friends for only a few short days, but nevertheless, the love and adoring admiration in the puppy's dark eyes promised to last a lifetime. What did it matter if Dick were leaving his home and the people and places he had always known, when such a friend as this was prepared to go across the whole world with him?

"You haven't a name," he said suddenly. "I am going to call you———"

"Cormac." A voice at his side startled him, for he had heard no sound of footsteps in the thick dust of the highroad. A rough-looking man, with a shock head and shifty, black eyes, stood staring at

CORMAC 41

the two. "Cormac, that's his name," he repeated. "See, he knows it."

The dog had cocked his ears, put his head on one side, and, sniffing cautiously, was coming closer to the stranger. He showed every sign of answering to his own name, but of distrusting the person who had spoken it.

"Is he—is he yours?" faltered Dick.

"Yes, he's mine," replied the other briefly, "but if you have taken a fancy to him, I'll sell him to you."

"For how much?" Dick said eagerly.

The man seemed to reflect. He looked the boy over and finally announced shortly, "Fifteen shillings." It was a staggering price to one who had his passage to America and provisions for the voyage still to pay for. The sovereigns that the sailor had paid to Dick were put away in the money belt under his clothes, and only a handful of silver coins were jingling in his pocket. He drew them out and counted them; there were twelve shillings in all.

"That's not enough," the man insisted. It was evident that he had guessed the love that already existed between these two and that the boy would give up anything rather than lose his cherished friend.

"If you don't want to buy him, we'll be off. Come here," he said roughly to the puppy.

The dog approached, slinking and drooping, then

suddenly drew back and bared his sharp puppy teeth in a snarl. The man aimed a kick at him with his heavy boot, but the alert Cormac jumped out of the way.

"He's not yours to sell," cried Dick.

"He isn't? Well, I'll just have the price of him anyway." The man seized Dick's hand that still held the shillings, wrenched open the boy's fingers, and pocketed the money. With one stride of his long legs he was over the gate in the hedge and stood grinning behind it.

"You're right, he isn't mine, but since I am three times your size, I don't see how you are going to get your money back. And I'll tell you the truth now, he belongs to John Brogan in the farmhouse over the hill yonder. If you take the dog away with you, it will be stealing him. But you had better take him, nobody will see you slip off with him, or ever be the wiser. That's the advice I give you in return for your twelve shillings."

He strode away along the path through the field, leaving Dick raging behind the gate. It was true that a boy of his size could not hope to force the great lout of a fellow to return his money. And what he had said made the boy stop to think. It was true he could take the dog away and no one would ever know. He had a moment of sore temptation. It seemed too hard that, for the price of twelve shillings that he could ill spare, he had bought the knowledge that Cormac's owner lived over the next hill. He knelt down in the dust and put his arms about the puppy's neck.

"There's nothing left to me in the world, not even you," he gulped. "I'll have to leave you behind. A—a man can't steal a friend."

The dog nuzzled his cheek and snuggled against his coat, then got up to follow unquestioning as Dick rose and turned into the lane that wound over the hill.

It was a comfortable farmhouse he came to, with wide barns and broad fields behind it, and with the master of the house himself dozing in the sun as he took his midday ease on the bench under the overhanging eaves. A little girl, probably about three years younger than himself, so Dick guessed, was sitting beside her father. She put down her very small square of sewing and sat staring at him with round, deep, blue eyes. Three puppies, too like Cormac to be anything but his brothers, came barking to the gate, and rolled and tumbled over their lost comrade with delight at his return. A magnificent collie, with a tremendous coat of red gold, here and there flecked with gray, lay in the sunshine beside his master's chair.

"Yes, he is mine," John Brogan said, in answer to Dick's question, while Cormac came wagging up to lick his hand and prove the truth of the statement. "This is his grandfather, a stiff old fellow now, but a great dog in his day. And his mother—there never was such a knowing one with the sheep. We named this puppy Cormac after the Irish king; that's Conall, his brother there, and the other is Rury."

He listened to Dick's story of how the dog had come to the cottage, of how that cottage came to be so empty, of how he had planned to take his new friend with him upon the long journey, and of what the man on the road had said and done.

"That would be like Tim Donahue," the farmer declared. "I turned him off for stealing the hens. I have always known he was a bad one. Probably he took your money and then advised you to steal the dog, as he would have done."

Dick made no answer, but stood looking down at Cormac, who had deserted his brothers and had come back to stand close against the boy's knee. John Brogan looked at them both reflectively.

"Going to America, are you?" he said slowly. "You are no great age or size, it seems to me, to be taking such a voyage."

"There seemed no place for me here," replied Dick. His voice sounded unsteady, so he said no more.

"And young Cormac here thought he would like to see America, too? Well, I wanted to see it myself when I was a young lad; but I never had the spirit to set off. You say you are going with Thomas Garrity? I know him; he will look after you, but you will have to learn how to get along with him." He paused and thought deeply again, while Dick felt his knees begin to shake.

The little girl touched her father's arm and spoke for the first time.

"Let him keep Cormac," she pleaded. "Can't you see how they love each other? And the boy hasn't anything else to love except Thomas Garrity."

The farmer smiled, apparently at the last thought.

"Cormac is of good stock," he said, "and he will be a valuable dog some day. But I would not be the one to stand in the way of his going where I would once have liked to go myself. Take the dog and go on your way, and may every kind of good luck go with you. I think you will need it."

Dick's face beamed with such utter delight that the farmer laughed and refused to listen to his faltering words of thanks.

The little girl followed the boy to the gate and spoke shyly—

"You must—must not be surprised at Thomas Garrity. He is not like other people. He takes me on his knee and tells me stories. He will tell them to you, too; though you will not think so at first."

"Thank you, I will like that," replied Dick, although he scarcely heeded what she said, so happy was he in the possession of Cormac.

But as she stood looking up at him, he thought he had never seen such earnest or such friendly eyes. She spoke again in her shy little voice.

"If you and Cormac come back from America some day and—and happen to pass this way, you might stop to tell us how you fared."

"I will," Dick assured her, and felt suddenly that he would never forget her eager little face. She did not speak again, but stooped suddenly, kissed Cormac on the nose, turned, and ran back to the house.

When the two came out upon the highroad, a tall, two-wheeled cart was creaking its slow way past. Its burly driver, a man from Dick's own village, stopped and offered them a ride. The boy and the dog curled up happily together in the straw behind the high seat.

"I'll get you to the port by sundown," the carter assured him. "You'll have to go aboard your ship to-night, for I hear she's to sail with the morning tide. Rest easy there in the straw; me and Molly, that's the horse, will have you there in time."

The cart jolted; the great wheels squeaked, while Dick lay back in the straw with his arm close about Cormac, and watched the fields and hedgerows swim in the hot spring sunshine. He was very weary and might have fallen asleep had it not been for the thrill that went tingling through him each time he thought of the carter's words, "Your ship sails with the morning tide."

CHAPTER V

BENDEMEER'S STREAM

DICK lay on his back on the ship's deck, supposed to be sleeping, but in reality wide awake and staring up at the starry arch of the midnight sky. It was just such a soft spring night as the one when he had found the silver sixpence, although now there was no moon. Above him hung the same blue-white star that, at this season, always stood just over the rough chimney of the cottage at home. Now it was above the tip of the towering mast that pointed to it as the ship stood steady for a moment at the crest of each wave. A rope creaked monotonously in a block, as the sail tugged at it with every heave of the vessel. There was the same dip and splash, minute after minute, as the bow dropped to a coming wave, rose to breast it, and dropped again. As he lay under his tall rooftree of towering white sails with the canopy of stars above, he thought wonderingly of the tiny, low, thatched cottage that had been his home somewhere back there beyond the horizon, and he felt that it was as unreal and as far away as that new country toward which he was going.

The kindness of one of the ship's officers had permitted his sleeping on deck, on the excuse that he should be with the sheep. For the first part of the voyage the weather had been very unlike what it was to-night, so that he had lain day after day in the close air below, sick and supremely miserable. But now new life seemed to have come to him with the warm spring air, and he was almost happy, for the moment, with the mild breezes about him, with the kindly stars overhead, and with Thomas Garrity, so he felt certain, asleep in his bunk below.

Thomas Garrity! Dick scarcely knew yet what to think of him. The sailor had assuredly been right, for Dick knew Thomas Garrity the moment he saw him on the dock. The boy had come down the steep, cobbled street of the little town, which was no very great port, but which was, just the same, a strange and exciting place to him. Across the blossoming gardens he could see tall masts and spars at the end of every street and, here and there, a great, white sail being hoisted.

When he came out upon the pier alongside of which lay his ship, he saw a group of men helping to get the sheep aboard. No easy task, this seemed to be, for the bewildered creatures were running in all directions at once. A tall, broad-shouldered man who had been giving orders, turned and showed a face that made Dick's heart sink. It was lean and stern and hard, with deep lines about the mouth and with steel-blue eyes overhung by heavy, frowning brows. It was quite true that there was something about him unlike other men, so that this could be no one but Thomas Garrity.

"So you are the boy?" he said, after looking Dick over for a full minute. "You are not so big as I was looking for."

To this there seemed no encouraging reply to make, so Dick made none. He could not deny his age and size.

"And a dog, too?" went on the man. "Do you expect him to go with us?"

The big ram, a long-legged, awkward creature, with no horns, but with a hard forehead eager for butting, had, at this moment, broken through the barrier of two men's legs and was making off up the dock. With a delighted yelp, Cormac raced in pursuit.

"He'll be in the water," shouted some one, but the quick dog had headed him off and returned him to the flock.

"Maybe he can work his passage," Thomas Garrity conceded. "But how about you? Do you ever speak?"

Such a question made Dick feel more dumb than

BENDEMEER'S STREAM   51

ever, but he managed to get out a word or so to explain that his sailor friend had thought he was big enough to help with the sheep.

"Well, it is a long voyage and you will maybe be bigger when we get to the end of it," returned Thomas Garrity. "And as for your passage, I'll pay it halfway across, and after we have got that far, you can go on or turn back, just as it pleases you."

"But, but——" Dick protested, then realized from the chuckle of one of the men behind him that Thomas Garrity, with his grim, unchanging face, was getting off a joke at his expense. "I can pay the other half myself," he declared.

"Then begin earning your way now, you and your dog," said the other briefly. "Don't stand there gaping while that lamb is looking for its mother. It's this first half of the voyage that I am paying for."

This was not a hopeful beginning, nor, as time went on, did things go better. Dick remembered that, while he was so utterly and wretchedly seasick, he had once or twice opened his eyes and had seen Thomas Garrity bending over him with a look that had less harshness than at first and almost a little pity. But when he spoke, it was only to ask if the boy thought that his passage had been paid for him "to take his ease below, when the sheep were needing him." Poor Dick, miserable beyond words, could only turn his head away and refuse to answer.

The uneasy weather of the first week had ended in a storm that Dick would surely long remember. He had finally struggled on deck, resolved to breathe the fresh air again, even though the ship was still rolling and pitching. The sullen gray of the choppy sea looked sickeningly dreary, while a heavy bank of clouds on the horizon, showing black against the gray of the sky, looked not only dreary, but menacing.

"There's wind in those clouds," said one of the sailors. Dick wondered what he called the stiff breeze that was singing through the rigging overhead, but he thought it better to ask no questions. Cormac crawled along beside him, very limp and bedraggled, for dogs can be as seasick as humans. The two curled up together in a miserable heap against the bulwarks and paid no attention to the cold spray that came splattering over them.

Almost without interest he watched the black clouds overspread the gray ones and listened to the voice of the wind as it rose suddenly from a far-off roar to a scream of fury, and fell upon the staggering ship. There was, to his ears, a confusion of orders, of hurrying feet, of hastily lowered sails and rattling blocks, yet he cared little and moved less, even when the sailors, running back and forth, almost trod upon him. Then of a sudden he and Cormac leaped to their feet, roused to life at the same instant by a mishap that really concerned them.

A lurch of the ship had thrown the big ram against the side of the pen with such force that the bars broke and the whole flock of sheep came tumbling and scattering across the deck. They slid across the wet boards; they got between the sailors' legs; they tangled their own legs in the dragging ropes and were jerked this way and that. The dog and the boy raced back and forth, slipping also in the wet, falling foul of the ropes, vainly trying to drive their frightened charges together. Not one of the sailors had a moment to lend a hand; Thomas Garrity was below; so Dick and Cormac struggled alone with the wildly frightened and bleating flock.

More by the lurching of the ship than by the efforts of the boy and the dog, the sheep finally gathered into a panic-stricken gray-white huddle near the stern. There was a pause of a second during which Dick drew a breath of relief that was cut short in the middle. A huge wave, clawing over the rail, caught up one of the stragglers at the edge of the group and carried it overboard. By some instinct that was quicker than thought, Dick recollected that where one sheep goes, its comrades all will follow. He had gone with Michael More, once, to help him drive a flock to market and had never forgotten how, on a narrow bridge, one sheep had been crowded through the rail and had fallen into the shallow stream, and how half of the rest had jumped after it before Michael could stop them.

He plunged through the struggling, frightened crowd and flung himself against the bulwarks where the luckless beast had gone over. He shouted, he beat back the woolly forms that fought to pass over him. He was knocked off his feet, but was up again in a moment, determined to stop them at any cost. If only he were bigger, he thought despairingly. He seemed to be smothered in sheep, so many were they and so frantically bent upon destroying themselves.

Cormac, with never a sound, was fighting as furiously as his master, biting at legs, leaping against shoulders, knocked over and trampled upon a dozen times, but always up again to battle more fiercely than ever.

Then Dick was aware, all at once, of a big presence beside him, of a broad figure that stood immovable against the frightened onrush, and of a huge voice which carried above the sound of the struggle and of the storm, yet still spoke calmly.

"There, there," said Thomas Garrity, "quiet, my dears, be quiet, will you now."

It seemed that the sheep knew his voice and harkened to it, even in their desperate terror. The heaving mass quieted and spread apart; the big ram backed off from the bulwarks and limped away. The bleating ewes allowed themselves to be led or driven back to their proper place amidships, so that in no more than a few moments the danger was over and the sheep back in their pen. Cormac sat down on the deck, with his tongue hanging out and with the blood running from the edge of his ear where the ram had stepped on it.

"Which of all of you is hurt the most?" asked Thomas Garrity. "I think it is the ram. Lend me a hand with him here. It looks as if his shoulder was broken."

The big sheep was, however, only lame and bruised, as a brief inspection proved. Cormac's injuries were slight and, "You're whole, I see," was all that Thomas Garrity seemed to have to say of Dick's battered condition.

Later, however, when the ship's carpenter had made the pen safe once more, when the wind had dropped a little and the ship was steady on her course again, Thomas Garrity relaxed enough to say gruffly, "It was not so badly done, lad, though it would have been better had you been bigger."

The ungracious praise stung Dick, but he made no angry retort as he was tempted to do. "I am sorry we lost a sheep. I don't know which one it was that went over," was all he said.

"It was the oldest ewe. She was a good creature, with a face like a gentle old woman."

The regretful tenderness of the man's tone made Dick look at him in puzzled curiosity. It was, indeed, hard to know what to make of Thomas Garrity.

After the storm had passed, the weather turned to warm, sunny days with just enough breeze to carry them well upon their way. Dick and Cormac were on deck every waking moment now, and had forgotten their unhappy period of seasickness. It was then that Thomas Garrity devised a new form of torment. He ceased talking to Dick in the pleasant, homely Gaelic to which the boy was used, saying that it was time he practiced at speaking English. He made grim, sour jokes at the boy's awkward speech, and generally refused to listen when Dick slipped back into his accustomed tongue. The man's own talk was carefully free from Irish brogue, as though he had tried to leave not only Ireland, but her speech and ways, behind him. Sometimes the accent of the words sounded Irish, never the words themselves. Dick, in learning English, came unconsciously to speak like him, although it was long before haste and excitement did not drive him back into his old tongue.

Sometimes he comforted himself by speaking Gaelic in a whisper to the sheep, who seemed to enjoy it as much as he, and who pushed against the bars of the pen, and breathed soft sighs of pleasure as he rubbed their warm noses. He had been talking to them thus to-night, as he lay close beside them, with Cormac curled up against his arm, a comfortable, sleepy bundle of fur.

His heart was swelling with black rage against Thomas Garrity and his unfailing harshness. Was he to spend months, years perhaps, in the company of such a man? Never! He would run away from him the minute they touched America. But how was he to endure even the rest of the voyage?

A sudden drowning flood of homesickness went over him, of longing for what was past, of sick terror for what might be to come. His own cottage, the loving friendliness of Bridget Anne and her husband, the kindness of the old spinning woman, the hearty greetings of the village folk in the lane—they all shone warm and bright in his memory. And for the future there was nothing to think of but a new country, an empty wilderness, and Thomas Garrity. He could not—he would not bear it. He would take passage again the moment he reached port and go back to Ireland. He had a wild dream that some vessel might speak their ship in mid-ocean, and take him aboard to carry him home. He would tramp through the village in the dusk, with Cormac at his heels; he would come back to his cottage where the sailor would be sitting by the fire; he would knock at the door——

What had the sailor said? "Wherever you go you must take your courage with you." And was Dick showing courage now? Was not this one of the times when "if you turn one way, it's bad, and if you turn another, it's worse, and there's nothing to do but go forward." Finn McCoul had gone forward, but—ah—he was going toward Ireland!

Dick fought against the clutching homesickness; he made himself face the fact that he could not go home from America, for he had not the passage money, he could not stay in his own village, for there was no one who would have him. So he must go on. "Hold up your head, and that will hold up your heart." Could he do that? He could. It was strange how differently he felt after he had made his resolution. He drew Cormac closer to him and closed his eyes for sleep. A moment later, however, he opened them and sat up to listen, for he thought he heard some one singing.

He had listened to the sailors singing at their work, he had heard Bridget Anne and others of the village people singing in the dusk of summer evenings, he had once, even, been taken to the great church in the nearest big town and had heard the choir chanting, and a boy with a voice like an angel singing alone. But he had never heard a voice like this, full and steady and true, that presently rose in the silence and filled the soft, warm night with melody. The song was one he had heard many a time, and it seemed to hurt his heart with the thrilling beauty of its simple music.

> "There's a bower of roses by Bendemeer's stream,
>   And the nightingales sing round it all the day long,
> In times of my childhood 'twas like a sweet dream,
>   To sit by the roses and hear the birds' song."

Who could sing so, who could melt all the strength within him with longing for home? Someone, surely, who was as homesick as himself. The voice deepened in the richer music of the next lines.

> "That bower and its roses, I'll never forget,
>   For often in spring and the bloom of the year
> I think are the nightingales singing there yet,
>   And the roses still bright by the calm Bendemeer."

"The bloom of the year." That was the season at which he had said good-by to Ireland. It was in such beauty of blooming flowers and new green leaves and soft winds heavy with fragrance that he would always remember her. Even the singer's voice had choked a little over the words. Dick stole out of the shadow and came full upon the man who sat leaning against a coil of rope, lifting his voice to the sea and the stars. It was Thomas Garrity!

He might not have known what to do had it not been for Cormac. The dog had followed him and now went close, curled up against the side of the big man, and dropped his nose on his paws with a sigh of sleepy content. Dick crept to the other side, sat down close beside Thomas Garrity, and whispered—"Go on." The peace of the night, the beauty of the music, and the sudden knowledge that his harsh master was longing for Ireland even as he did himself, had put an end to all fear.

"No, the roses soon withered that hung o'er the wave,
But some blossoms were gathered while freshly they shone,
And a dew was distilled from their flowers that gave
All the fragrance of summer when summer was gone.

"Thus memory draws from delight ere it dies
An essence that breathes of it many a year;
Thus bright to my soul as 'twas then to my eyes,
Is that bower by the banks of the calm Bendemeer."

Dick drew a deep, tremulous breath and came so close that he was, unaccountably, within the circle of Thomas Garrity's great arm. Neither spoke for a moment after the song came to an end, until Cormac stirred, changed his position, and sighed sleepily again.

"It doesn't do to look back too much, lad," said a voice that he hardly knew as Thomas Garrity's. "There are roses, too, beside the river where we are going, and who knows, we may learn to love that new land as we have loved our old one."

He spoke in Gaelic, to Dick's great content. The

BENDEMEER'S STREAM

fact gave the boy courage to put a question that, in his ignorance, he had long wished to ask.

"Why must I always speak English to you? Is there no one who talks in Gaelic in the new country?"

"No one," his master assured him, "so that a boy is lost and helpless who speaks only that tongue. When once you have learned English, we will talk together in Gaelic again. But in America, every one speaks in English except the Indians."

Indians! He had heard of them vaguely, as beings as far off and unreal as the Little People themselves. Less real, indeed, for had he not heard stories of the fairies every day of his life, but very few of the shadowy, copper-colored creatures who slipped without sound through the dense forest, hunting and fishing and leading strange lives far beyond the boundary of anything he could imagine. Were they really as cruel as some of the tales of them declared? Or were they only magic, mischievous beings like the leprecauns and the imps of Bridget Anne's stories? It was so he imagined them.

Would they be standing on the shore when the ship came into harbor, he inquired.

Thomas Garrity seemed to be thinking of other things and brought back his attention with an effort.

"Will who—oh, the Indians? No, you must go many miles from the sea, now, to find them, for they have been driven back into the wilderness."

Dick nodded. That was like the Little People, too, who shrank away from the overcrowded haunts of men.

"We will put in at Philadelphia, the port our ship is bound for," Thomas Garrity went on, "and we will cross the state of Pennsylvania, which is bigger than Ireland, and as green. Then we will come to mountains, steep and rugged and covered with woodland. Those mountains we will climb. We will look down upon a silver, winding river, bigger than any you have ever seen before. That river we will follow. And then we will come to something of which you never even dreamed, a river so great that you will think it must be a portion of the sea, except for its warm blue, and for the current that runs swifter than the tide, but always one way. That river we will cross and find beyond it the wilderness and the Indians and the wide, green meadows, of which a man may have all he wants for the asking. I have chosen a spot for us to live, beyond the range of white men's settlements, where we will not be troubled by landlords and boundaries and acreages for many a year to come."

Dick could say nothing, but he listened, with quivering interest.

"We will live there and prosper and—fools that we are—we will sometimes be breaking our hearts to be back and starving in Ireland. But look you,

Dick, the world will be happier and less crowded when people begin to live in that new land, that is waiting for cattle and sheep and a plow to turn the fat, black furrows. Men are like sheep, they hang back from unknown things and follow where others have had the spirit to go first. The whole world, and Ireland with it, will be made better off by those who have courage to go into the wilderness."

Courage! Dick shivered a little at the thought that even Thomas Garrity had need to think of taking courage on his journey with him. But he was very comfortable against the big man's arm and, as he talked on, grew drowsier and drowsier. The stars moved past, one after another, out of sight beyond the curve of the sail, while the waves, in endless procession, went marching by, their hushed voices talking softly against the ship's side. The man looked down, smiled, and sat unmoving with the dog nestled against one side of him and the boy against the other, until the stars faded and the waves dropped in the stillness that comes with dawn.

CHAPTER VI

BURWICK FAIR

THE remainder of the voyage passed happily; for, although Thomas Garrity seemed to return next day to his harsh manner, Dick understood that within there was, as the sailor had said, a different man. There were more soft, warm evenings when the two sat on deck together, while Thomas Garrity told stories of Ireland. They were not tales like Bridget Anne's of the Little People or of saints and archangels, but stories of the old Irish kings and the great heroes of half-forgotten legends, who went forth to battle and adventure with their white horses, their flaunting banners, and their shining spears. In the daytime Thomas Garrity was still a stern taskmaster, but at night he put off his hardness of manner and unlocked for Dick the magic gates of legend and romance. Instead of longing with all his heart for the voyage to come to an end, the boy began to wish it might last forever.

They came to port, finally, on a hot day at the end of June. There were no Indians waiting on the shore to greet them, as Dick had once imagined, yet he found much to wonder at in the staid Quaker citizens of Philadelphia with their gray clothes and broad hats. He had never seen a city before, and, used as he was to the villages of tumbledown cottages in his own part of Ireland, he scarcely knew what to make of the clean, wide streets and the tidy rows of houses.

He had no great chance for observing the strangeness of the city, however, for he, Thomas Garrity, and Cormac all had full occupation in getting the sheep ashore, driving them the length of Market Street, and finally out upon the turnpike that led into green, open country.

It might seem a tedious journey to walk, at a sheep's pace, across the whole state of Pennsylvania, but to Dick, busy with attending to the flock and with seeing things new and interesting on every side, there was never a dull moment. Sometimes the road was hot and dusty, sometimes shaded by cool woods, sometimes climbing over the low, round hills, sometimes dipping to a green valley where ran some busy, clear-watered stream. They slept at farmhouses along the way, where there never failed a welcome from the prosperous Pennsylvania farmers who spoke such odd half-German English, and who had such big barns, such comfortable stone houses, and such wide, fertile fields.

All seemed to know Thomas Garrity; evidently he

had traveled that way more than once before. A very few seemed to have seen through his harsh outside and realized the gentleness of the man within, while every one respected him and spoke well of him.

"Why do you go on, when there is here all man could ask?" their hosts often inquired when the two adventurers, after a stop to rest and graze the sheep, were ready to be upon the road again.

"The settled country is not for me," Thomas Garrity would reply. Dick noticed that his mouth was set in grim lines as he spoke, as though at the memory of those sorrows which had driven him from Ireland, but which, in spite of himself, could not break his love for his own land. Dick, too, felt no temptation to linger; and even Cormac, running and barking to get his flock together, was always impatient to be off.

If Dick had grown on the voyage, which according to Thomas Garrity's prophecy he had, indeed, succeeded in doing, Cormac had accomplished even greater wonders in the same direction. From a round, soft puppy he had turned into a long-legged, half-grown dog, with a white ruff about his neck, with silky, dark ears, and a splendid brush of a tail. Even without the example of an older sheep dog, he seemed to know by instinct how to drive and herd his flock. It might have seemed to others that

Thomas Garrity and his sturdy assistant, Dick Martin, were driving twenty ewes, one great ram, and a handful of bleating lambs, born upon the voyage, westward toward the mountains. But the real truth of the matter, at least in one doggish brain, was that they were traveling as the sole charge and responsibility of an earnest, tawny-coated collie named Cormac.

They had gone three-fourths of their way across the State, when they were obliged to make a longer stop than at any time before. The big ram was in trouble. The injury to his shoulder on shipboard had resulted in a lameness that grew worse as the journey went on. Instead of marching at the head of the flock, with his head up and his bell swinging, he now lagged behind the others, with bent neck and dull eyes. At last Thomas Garrity declared he had not the heart to drive the suffering animal farther.

They were getting into the rougher country in the western part of the State and had stopped at a small farm that clung to a steep hillside. With its low-roofed cottage, its sheds of rough stone and its small fields, it was far less prosperous than the rich, German-owned farms they had been passing; but the owner, his cheerful wife, and their three white-headed children all seemed contented and happy. The two cows, the pigs, and the handful of sheep all seemed so well cared for that Dick felt sure that, if their poor ram must be left behind somewhere, it had better be here.

They stood in the heat of a still, midsummer afternoon looking down at the worn-out animal as he lay panting in the shade of a big tree. He drank gratefully of the water the children had brought him, but he could not touch the grass or grain they offered.

"I could not leave him in better hands than yours," said Thomas Garrity slowly to Hiram Evarts, the farmer, who seemed, like many others, to be an old acquaintance.

"I would buy him from you if I could," replied Hiram, looking down at the ram with kindness and pity on his weather-worn face, "but ready money is so rare with me that I cannot offer it. I will take good care of the poor beast, and when you come this way again, you shall have him back."

"There is not much chance I shall be taking him back again," said Thomas Garrity, "and I am glad to think how well he will fare amongst you. But where in the world am I to get another?"

The younger boy tugged at his father's coat and whispered something that he was too shy to speak aloud. Thomas Garrity caught one or two of the words and smiled his grimmest smile.

"Is it Anthony Robins I hear you naming?" he

asked. "Yes, I know him, and the sheep he raises, good sheep they are, but unfortunate in their master. I bought two from him three years ago, paying twice their value. I know more about sheep now, and much more about Anthony Robins, so I will never be likely to buy from him again."

"He has a ram that is the wonder of the whole county," observed Hiram, "and they say he is putting him up for sale at the fair over at Burwick."

"The ram butted Anthony Robins clean through the fence," put in the oldest boy, "so even he is afeard of the beast, people say, and that is why he is to be sold. He is the biggest sheep I ever saw and has horns like that."

He made a wide circle with his sun-burned hands to show the greatness of the creature's horns.

"And when his master comes to sell him, he will prize him as though he were the ram with the golden fleece," said Thomas Garrity. "No, I deal no more with Anthony Robins."

"They do say, hereabouts, that the two best men at buying and selling are Anthony Robins and Thomas Garrity," remarked the farmer, "and it has always been a question among us which could do better than the other. It's a trial to Anthony to hear anybody speak of it; for he cannot bear to believe any one is better at a bargain than himself. It is true he wants a great price for the ram; he is a big, beautiful creature, but a wicked one."

Dick spoke up at this.

"I should like to see him," he said.

"So you may," returned Hiram. "Burwick Fair is on your road westward and it begins to-morrow. We are all going ourselves. Not one of us but would feel cheated all the year should we miss the midsummer fair."

That evening, as they gathered in the deep porch of the farmhouse and watched the yellow moon come up, Dick and the children began to grow better acquainted. They told him of the work they did; for, with so much to be accomplished to wring a living for the five of them out of the tiny fields, there was a task for every minute of the day. But it was plain, as they talked of finding the nests of the yellow-breasted larks in the meadows, of watching for the first pink buds of the mountain laurel, of bringing in the round, white hickory nuts to crack beside the fire in winter, that they found their life an exciting as well as a busy one, and that they were all happy working together and for each other.

The little girl brought out their greatest treasure to show him. Even children who struggle with grown-up tasks must have their toys; nor were these children without theirs. During the long winter evenings their father had fashioned for them a

Noah's Ark, such a big one that it held more animals than Dick could name.

Hiram had carved them for his children out of soft pine and colored them from their mother's dye-tub. Reindeer and zebras, foxes and polar bears—the children knew them all as the little girl paraded them on the wide stone step. Even Hiram and Thomas Garrity put down their pipes to examine the animals that were strangest of all to Dick's eyes, antelope, elk, buffalo, and mountain lion.

"You will see these, where you are going," Hiram said to Dick, and the boy felt his blood run quicker at the thought.

"We want you to have one to take with you, to remember us by," the little girl declared. She hesitated long over the choice, for she and her brothers were united in the wish that Dick should have the best.

"You must take Mr. Noah," she decided at last; and a very gorgeous Mr. Noah it was, four inches high and wearing a red waistcoat, a green coat, and a yellow hat. Dick wrapped him carefully in a big red handkerchief and packed him away in his shabby bundle.

After he had lain down to sleep that night, he heard the children's mother moving about the house, on tired feet that had gone up and down since sunrise. In the morning he found that she had washed and ironed his travel-worn clothes, had mended the rents, and sewed on the buttons. She, also, had a small gift for him, a roll of leather, called a housewife, inside which were needles, thread, buttons, and a big horn thimble.

"You will be wondering some day where you will get more clothes," she said, "so do the best you can to make these you have hold together. And do not forget that buttons are rare and precious things where you are going."

There had been a hurt place in Dick's heart ever since that day when Peggy Reilly's sharp tongue had lashed him with the truth that no one wanted him. Now the last of that pain seemed to vanish at the sight of Elizabeth Evarts' tired, friendly smile.

It was necessary to set out before sun-up to be in time for Burwick Fair. Dick had expected some such a festive meeting as the fairs at home, where there was laughing and dancing, much drinking, and not a little fighting. Here matters were very different. Grave-faced old farmers, some Quakers, some broad-faced Germans, some small, lean Welshmen, hurried back and forth, absorbed in the important business of buying and selling. The younger men looked more alike than their elders, and were less evidently German, Welsh, or Scotch, and more American; yet even among them were quaint, square-toed shoes, full-skirted coats, and a general air of gravity. Their wives, except for the Quaker women, were in flowered bonnets, and the children in bright-colored dresses; but the women were talking of their butter and the children of their pet lambs or pigs, rather than looking for the excitement and merrymaking that Dick had always thought must belong to a fair. But there were everywhere broad shoulders, stout legs, round, rosy cheeks, and a general air of well-being.

He had never seen such sleek cattle, such thick-coated sheep, such stout, contented-looking pigs. He went from pen to pen, Hiram Evarts' oldest son going with him.

"There is Anthony Robins' ram," the bigger boy said at last, "and yonder is Anthony Robins himself."

Dick was more interested in the animal than in the man. He had certainly never seen such a ram. It was lying down at the moment, in the corner of the pen, but even thus he could see the breadth of its back, the strength of its big shoulders, and the beautiful sweep of its horns. He put his hand between the bars and touched the deep, close-growing wool. Once when he was very little, Bridget Anne had taken him to the great house of the neighborhood, and the housekeeper had let them go through some of the big, empty rooms, since the family was away. He remembered sticking his finger into the great, stuffed armchair in which the master of the house used to sit before the fire, and he thought now of that firm softness which was like the close, deep wool of the sheep's coat.

"Take care," cried his companion, as the big ram leaped to his feet with the agility of a cat and struck with his great horns against the side of the pen.

"He has been illtreated," said Dick. "Steady, steady, there's a good fellow. Nobody's going to harm you."

"What are you doing?" asked a grating voice at his elbow. The boy had scarcely noticed Anthony Robins, but he was forced to take account of him now.

He was small and bent, with shambling joints, and a face so ugly that he looked to Dick like an old and bad-tempered monkey.

"I'll not have you plaguing my sheep," the man went on. "That's a valuable animal and not to be —ah, Thomas Garrity, is it you?"

"It is I," returned Thomas Garrity, who had come up behind Dick.

"That is a fine sheep there," began the other at once, losing no time in scenting out the chance for a bargain, "and I am selling him cheap. A beautiful animal."

"With a beautiful disposition, I notice," answered Thomas Garrity. "Just lead him out of the pen, will you, and let me look him over."

"You can see him well enough from here," Anthony Robins answered sourly. "Rams don't sell for their dispositions. Look at his shoulders and that fleece. What will you give?"

The passing farmers stopped, waited to listen to what Thomas Garrity would offer, finally gathered in greater numbers and made a circle about the two. Bargaining was a great art amongst the shrewd country folk, and here were two famous antagonists met before a delighted audience. The crowd increased from all sides, and every man waited to hear what would develop. Thomas Garrity's firmness and sense of justice, Anthony Robins' obstinacy and greed—which would get the better of the other?

"I will give you fifty dollars," Thomas Garrity stated briefly. Dick could have sworn that Anthony Robins' lips had been ready to frame the word forty, but he saw them close hard at the generosity of the other's offer.

"Sixty," he announced, "and the beast is worth double."

"I have bought sheep from you before, and I have learned what prices you put upon them," Thomas Garrity said. "I had vowed I would never buy of you again, but need presses me, and I like your ram. I will give you fifty dollars, as I said."

"Not one penny less than sixty will I take," replied Anthony Robins. "He is of the best breed in Pennsylvania."

"And the worst temper," Thomas Garrity added.

"I have brought him up from a lamb." There was a sentimental whine in the other's voice. "I would never be willing to sell him, only——"

"Only you beat and abused him until now he has grown so fierce that you are afraid of him."

"That is false." To prove the docility of the animal he was trying to sell, Anthony Robins leaned over the pen and rapped the ram's forehead with his knuckles.

It was a most unwise move. Dick saw the big beast's eyes flash red with rage and hatred, as the ram, with a snort and a plunge, was half through, half over, the pen, and a moment later was pursuing his master through the scattering, dodging crowd. There was no danger to any of the bystanders, however, for the furious animal was intent only upon overtaking his special enemy. Once he knocked him sprawling and then backed off, stamping his hoofs and shaking his horns, waiting for the dazed victim to get up and be knocked down again.

In the midst of the green before the sheepshed

was a flagstaff, tall and stout, which had so recently been a forest tree that it still showed knobs and bumps where once the branches had been. Up this scrambled Anthony Robins with the agility of the monkey he so closely resembled. There he clung, a small, ignominious figure, but still obstinate.

"Sixty dollars, Thomas Garrity," he shrieked.

"Fifty," repeated Garrity with unmoved face.

Anthony Robins stared down ruefully at the ram, waiting below. It was plain that no man could cling forever to the slippery flagpole and that the matter must be speedily brought to some end. He looked despairingly about him upon the crowd.

"I will sell him to any man of you for forty dollars," he cried. "To Thomas Garrity my price is sixty, for he shall never say that he got the best of me at a bargain. But think—forty dollars for a fine beast like that. Any one of you should be glad to buy him."

Crash, the ram's heavy horns struck the base of the flagstaff, shaking it from the summit to the ground. The small man almost dropped from his perch, but still he clung frantically.

"Forty dollars," he wailed again.

"The creature will kill you when you come down," Thomas Garrity assured him, "and come down you must in time."

There was a long pause.

"Silas Green," said Robins at last, desperately, "go and get that rifle that I saw in your wagon—and shoot this mad beast. It is true he means to kill me, if I come down. And I would rather have him killed than give in to Thomas Garrity. Unless——" And once more he looked beseechingly over the crowd. "Unless one of you will buy him, I will sell him for thirty-five dollars."

There was another long pause. It was not strange that no one seemed disposed to buy.

"Silas Green, go fetch your gun," Anthony Robins ordered again. And the long man in blue jeans shambled off to do his bidding.

"I will give you thirty-four dollars."

Dick's voice, even in his own ears, sounded very high and thin as he lifted it up before that crowd of strangers.

His delay in making the offer was only because he had been hastily counting his money and trying, with wits whirling from excitement, to calculate what the pounds and shillings would be in dollars. The sailor's sovereigns had dwindled and dwindled; the very small wages Thomas Garrity could afford to pay had added very little to the sum; so that thirty-four dollars was the total of all Dick had. Yet he had no hesitation in offering it, when otherwise that beautiful, bold creature must be killed.

"Done," returned Anthony Robins, relief struggling with greed in his tone, "although it is much too little. Pay your money to Silas Green there, he will receive it for me, and now come and take your animal away. But Thomas Garrity is not to help you, or the bargain is at an end."

This time Dick hesitated. It was not from fear of the great ram who stood defying the whole multitude with his magnificent horns lowered, and with the sun like silver on his close, white coat. The boy dreaded far more the circle of strangers' eyes, all watching him, all waiting to see how he would acquit himself.

He heard a Quaker woman close to him say to her husband:

"Couldn't thee help the boy, Phineas?"

"No, Rachel," the man answered, "we must see first what the lad can do alone."

Dick had never felt so little or so young as when he whistled to Cormac and walked out upon the empty green.

CHAPTER VII

THE SHINING ROAD

IN the curious way in which animals seem able to tell things to each other, Cormac managed to make the big ram understand that here were friends. He paid no attention to the menacing horns, but came up, stepping daintily on his slim, white feet, sniffed, and stood still while the excited creature sniffed cautiously in return. Dick knelt down on the grass and waited, while the ram came slowly up to him and ran an investigating nose down his sleeve. Some unknown person—it may have been the Quaker woman, it may have been Hiram Evarts' small daughter who had proudly carried a little basket of her own show vegetables to the fair—had thrust a handful of carrots into his pocket. The sniffing nose of the big sheep found them out, nibbled at one, and drew it slowly forth. He sampled another, then came closer, dropped his great head, and rubbed it against the boy's shoulder. Cormac looked around at the spectators and laughed as only a collie can laugh, with ears and tail and delighted, expressive face.

THE SHINING ROAD 81

The big sheep's sides were still heaving, and he started back as a roar of applause went up from the crowd. But the wild glint faded from his eyes as Dick's comforting hand patted his neck, and the three, the boy with his face beaming, the dog with his tail wagging, and the sheep with the feathery green of the last carrot sticking out of his mouth, came together across the green to Thomas Garrity.

Behind them Anthony Robins slid down the pole and went quickly to count the money that Silas Green handed to him. The bargain was concluded. It was not, however, to be the end of Dick's intercourse with Anthony Robins.

The family of Hiram Evarts stood in a group at the crossroads to wave good-by to Dick and Thomas Garrity as they set off once more upon their journey. The sun was hot and the highway deep in dust, which rose under the sheep's feet into a choking cloud as they moved along. Dick, however, minded neither the heat nor the dust, for was not that his very own ram who walked at the head of the little procession, with head high and with proudly stepping feet, the haughty leader of the flock.

They had journeyed possibly five miles beyond Burwick, when they heard hoofbeats on the road and were overtaken by a great gray carthorse, mounted by a small rider, who bounced high with every jog of the broad back and who was, unmistakably, Anthony Robins.

He reined up as he came close to them, wiped his heated, dusty face, and addressed Thomas Garrity.

"I hear you left a ram with Hiram Evarts. I know that fellow could not give you any decent price for him, if he gave any. I will buy the beast, worn-out as I understand he is, if you can be reasonable as to what you want for him."

Thomas Garrity, instead of answering, lifted his hand and laid it upon the horse's neck. The great animal jumped and shied, almost unseating his rider.

"There is no creature that belongs to you, Anthony Robins," he said, "that does not flinch when one touches him, because he knows of nothing but blows. No animal of mine shall ever come into your hands."

"But if I offer you——"

"We will name no prices. You would not sell me your ram; you may be sure I will not sell you mine."

Thomas Garrity swung on his heel and walked on, driving the sheep before him, but Anthony Robins stopped Dick as he would have followed.

"Pull up that strap of my stirrup, will you, boy?" he said. And as Dick did as he was asked, the little man leaned from the saddle and spoke earnestly.

"I know that country whither Thomas Garrity is taking you, and I consider it only friendly to warn you before it is too late. Your comrade has perhaps made you think it is a place of romance and adventure, but do not believe him. Your life will be harder than anything you ever dreamed off; you will be always hungry and in winter always cold. You will labor so hard to keep alive that you will often wonder why you do not lie down and die for very weariness. Oh, I have seen it, I have been there, and was wise enough to come away again."

He had set his horse forward at a foot pace, while Dick walked beside him, listening, in spite of himself, to what the man had to say.

"But the big, wide rivers—the new lands—the Indians——" the boy faltered.

"Great, cruel rivers, that in their flood-time sweep over the whole neighboring country," Anthony Robins described them briefly. "Flat lands with nothing but grass and trees along the watercourses, and never the sight of a house or a barn or a comforting church steeple. And the Indians—what do you expect from them—dirty, treacherous beings as they are? One day you will think they are your friends and the next you will be lying dead in the brush with the painted feathers of an arrow standing out between your ribs. That will be your end unless some frontier pestilence strikes you down with its deadly sickness first."

Anthony Robins checked his horse and turned him about in the road.

"I could find a place on my farm for a sturdy boy like you," he remarked carelessly, "and you would not have to leave all this." He waved his hand toward the wide, green landscape of fertile fields, white roads, and, here and there, clusters of farm buildings. "You will lead a pleasant and prosperous life here, while there——" He did not finish the sentence, leaving the possible future to Dick's imagination.

"Will you stay?" he concluded abruptly.

Dick shook his head. "I must see the new country," he answered.

"Well, I have done my best to warn you," the other returned, "and I will give you one more word of advice, if you will go on. See the new country, and then come away. Sell the lands you have settled on, to some fool who will come after you and who knows as little of the wilderness as you do now. That is the only profit of any sort that you will get, and a small one it will probably be. It was what I did; I sold out for scarcely twice what I put in, and I lost a whole, good year of my life while I was doing it."

THE SHINING ROAD   85

He kicked his mount in the ribs and jogged away as he had come, a small, ridiculous figure on the great, clumsy horse.

Thomas Garrity asked no questions when Dick rejoined him. The two journeyed on in almost complete silence for the rest of the day, since their hot, dry throats made talking difficult, and since they had all they could do to keep the sheep from turning off the dusty roads into the inviting green of the fields.

The hills they climbed became steeper and steeper, the country more barren, and the farms fewer on either hand. On the third night they stopped near the top of a ridge and slept in the open, since there was no convenient place to ask for lodging. Dick, Cormac, and the big ram—inseparable friends now, the three of them—lay close together in the shadow of a big bowlder. The sky was clear overhead, with the midsummer brightness of the Milky Way stretching from horizon to horizon. Dick's familiar, blue-white star had moved past the zenith and was hanging lower in the west. The night was still and warm; the flock was quiet; but Dick could not sleep.

He sat up at last, with his arm around his knees, thinking earnestly. For the first time, all the warnings that Anthony Robins had uttered came flooding into his mind. He had paid little attention to the man who so plainly hated Thomas Garrity, who had been trying to reverse his own defeat by attempting, first to get possession of Thomas Garrity's ram, and then to lead away his comrade. But still there might have been some truth in what he said. A hard, cruel life, he had described it, with treacherous rivers and treacherous Indians. And he had been there!

He looked up suddenly and saw the tall figure of his companion standing motionless beside the great rock, looking across toward the top of the ridge. Away to the east the moon was coming up, a late, one-sided moon, that was drowning the near-by stars in its white light.

"Well?" said Thomas Garrity. It seemed as though he read the boy's thoughts, but would say no word to still his doubts

Dick looked up at him and smiled. Whatever the future might hold, he felt ready now to go to the world's end with Thomas Garrity. His comrade smiled in return.

"Come with me," he said. "Bid Cormac lie still, and step softly so that the sheep will stay quiet. There is something I should like to show you."

They walked together to the summit of the ridge and looked across it to the open country below. There, winding away toward the west, was a broad river, its course outlined by the dark trees along its bank, its smooth waters giving back the silver light of the moon. For unnumbered miles it turned and twisted and dwindled to a small, shining thread in the far distance.

"That is our road into the wilderness," said Thomas Garrity. "Shall we follow it—or go back?"

Dick laughed aloud in the stillness of the night.

"We will follow it," he answered.

Cormac and the big ram, aroused by his voice, came across the hill in the clear, white light to nuzzle at his hand and try to ask why their master was not asleep.

It was at the bustling little town of Pittsburgh, at the foot of the mountains and at the head of navigation on the big river that they stopped for two days to secure their outfit for the later journey. They had to buy guns, blankets, and ammunition, to lay in supplies of food for themselves and the sheep, and to arrange for the boat that was to carry them on their second voyage.

On all sides they were told that they were in great luck to arrive at just that time. The Ohio, sometimes a raging flood upon which boats scarcely dared to embark, sometimes a lazy, indolent stream that loved to deposit its burdens on every shoal and bar along its valley, was now, at moderately high water, in the best of all conditions to carry them on their journey. It was late in the season for such a stage of water, but a river will do as it chooses, and Dick and Thomas Garrity profited by ts caprice. The big flatboat on which they embarked the sheep pursued its steady way day after day, around the sweeping curves, and past wooded shores, wild, green meadows, and scattered farms.

It was a very different journey from the laborious travel across Pennsylvania, for now there was no dust, no weary trudging at the sheep's heels, only a halt now and then to graze the flock, or for Dick to run along the shore to give exercise to his own restless legs and Cormac's. Dick's face grew browner and browner in the hot sun, and his muscles harder, as he helped to steer the big boat, or to pull at the great sweeps of oars. The boatmen told him strange tales of the river and the wilderness, some of them so conflicting that in the end, he scarcely knew what to believe.

"The way that the new world looks to you depends upon the eyes with which you see it," Thomas Garrity said to him at last. "These men like fighting and adventure, and they find them. Anthony Robins found hard work and hardship where he had thought to make much money from sharp bargaining with the Indians; he fared ill, and has talked sourly of the frontier life ever since."

"Are the Indians as—as treacherous as he says?"

THE SHINING ROAD

Dick ventured to ask. It was the first time he had ever spoken of Anthony Robins' warnings.

"They are if you deal treacherously with them, as many a white man thinks he can. But I will not try to explain the Indians to you. If you are ever to understand them you must learn to do so of yourself. A man must carry a steadfast heart and he must walk alone, when he goes into the wilderness, even a man the age of you, Dick Martin."

He was silent for a moment, watching the low, green shore slip quietly by, and then added—

"You must not forget that the first men in a new country are making history and that the eyes of their own time and of future days are on them. You have to go forward alone, but the world is watching you, that overcrowded world back beyond the mountrains, beyond the sea, where there is no longer quite enough room or quite enough food or quite enough human kindness for all."

As the days went on, more than one person said to him, "If you think this river is big, you must be ready to see a bigger." And one old boatman, tugging at the oar beside him, said—

"If your heart turns over inside you, when you see the Mississippi, then you will know you are the man for the wilderness."

They came out upon it at twilight, sliding out of the Ohio into what seemed to Dick a vast, shadowy sea. The flat shore opposite was hardly visible through the dusk, and the muddy waters looked gray in the half light. It was not beautiful, this first glimpse of the great river; but the broad stream was so huge, so quiet, so steadily moving, and yet so unhurried in its gigantic strength, that Dick felt a strange flutter inside as though his heart had indeed turned over within him. The Mississippi was like nothing that he had expected or had ever seen before.

It was a heart-breaking task to breast the swirling current and to drag the heavy boat up the long miles intervening between the Ohio and St. Louis. Fortune still favored them, however, for a fair wind filled their clumsy sail, and carried them forward for the greater part of the way. When they reached St. Louis, it was necessary to load the sheep on smaller boats for the shallower waters of the upper Mississippi. Then began what seemed to Dick the most toilsome portion of the whole journey. By rowing, by poling, by spreading sail when they could catch a favorable wind, they made their way against the unwilling river that seemed to be exerting all its strength to sweep them back and down to the sea.

They could not even travel straight upstream, but wove their way back and forth between the shores, following the intricate channel. Nor could

THE SHINING ROAD

their pilot be sure of the shifting way, so that more than once one or the other of the three boats stuck fast on reefs or the ends of sloping sandbars. In such a case every man must go overboard and tug and push at the grounded boat until she was afloat again. Dick was so weary that he scarcely noticed that the flat banks were rising to higher and steeper wooded bluffs, that the water was growing ever clearer and bluer, and that the threads of smoke, here and there marking a solitary settler, were becoming more and more infrequent. He did, however, mark the growing anxiety in Thomas Garrity's face that became more troubled, day by day. Time was passing, and it was of the greatest importance that they should reach their journey's end before the autumn began.

It was the end of August now. The breathless heat hung heavy on the river by day, and seemed to abate little when they camped at night.

"You should be thankful for the good weather," the boatmen said—a rougher-dressed and rougher-mannered crew than the one that had brought them down the Ohio—"We'll get you to the Des Moines, we hope, before this fair spell breaks."

Finally, one clear, hot afternoon, they rounded to in the mouth of a tributary river on the west side of the Mississippi. The willow-fringed banks of the smaller stream lifted to green, open meadows and these, in turn, rose to steep, wooded hills. The bluffs at either side of the river's mouth were high and rocky, like the pillars of a great gate. Through the portal their boats came into the quieter current of the Des Moines; where the water was low enough to show white sandbars; where here and there a lazily floating log washed up and grounded. The feathery branches of the willows stirred softly, swinging aside to give glimpses of cool, dark shade between their close trunks.

The boats came slowly to shore at an opening in the trees where the green meadows ran down to the water's edge. Cormac leaped ashore, the big ram jumped after him, and the sheep followed pellmell. Dick forgot his stiff legs and aching muscles as he jumped after them. The long journey had really come to an end.

The supplies were landed and carried up the bank: the men on being paid, went back almost immediately to their boats.

"I got you here before the weather broke," grinned the chief boatman, "but not much before. There's going to be a big storm presently. We'll have time to get out into the Mississippi and drop below the point before it comes. I'd like to get that far on the way back before she strikes. That must be an Indian village up yonder, where you see the smoke. I wouldn't go near it for a day or two, if I were you. Give the Indians time to look you over, like."

One boat and then another pushed out into the stream, but he stood with his foot on the bow of the last one, as its stern swung restlessly in the current.

"I'll be back in the spring according to arrangement, to bring you in supplies and take your wool to St. Louis. Next May, did you say? Yes, I'll see you then—if you are still here. Well, so long."

He stepped aboard, swung out into the river, and was gone. So this was really the end—and the beginning. The last link that bound Dick and Thomas Garrity to civilization was snapped. They were buried in the wilderness, with no road back to the settled country save that unknown highway of the mighty river.

From where he stood Dick could look up the valley where the flat green of the bottom lands stretched away, and where the wooded hills came together in the blue distance. The Des Moines had cut its channel at the foot of the southern bluff, leaving miles of open, level country, as smooth and verdant as a garden. Scattered trees showed the dark green of oaks and the slim lines of elms, while the soft yellow-green of the willows fringed the shore of the river as far as the eye could see. Two miles away a thin column of smoke, going straight up in the hot, still air, marked the site of the Indian village.

A bank of clouds to the westward, piling up above the distant hills, were messengers of the coming storm. The air grew hotter and heavier; the clouds, blue-black, and purple, came rolling up across the sky.

"The rain will be here in an hour," Dick thought, and at that instant, heard a strange, rushing wind beginning to blow. The oaks bowed their heads before it; the elm trees flung out their arms; the willows along the bank suddenly bent almost to the ground under its growing fury and the white lash of the rain. A heavy roll of thunder went echoing along the hills.

Thomas Garrity was hastily throwing the sheets of canvas over the heap of ammunition and supplies that had been unloaded from the boat. At the first sound of thunder the sheep broke and ran for cover in the willows and were followed a moment later by Thomas Garrity, driven by the stinging fury of the rain. Dick who was higher up the slope, sought refuge in the more open woods upon the hillside where he was joined by Cormac, a wet, bedraggled Cormac, who hid his head on his master's breast and whimpered with terror of the thunder rolling overhead.

Never had they heard such thunder. It growled;

THE SHINING ROAD

it crackled; it roared; it ran from end to end of the black sky. Then it hung directly above them, breaking forth in one deafening clap after another, while the blinding strokes of lightning whipped earth and sky in every direction. Dick saw a great, round, oak tree suddenly struck, flung asunder and thrown to the ground in a shower of flying splinters, but with the noise of its downfall drowned by an overwhelming crash in the sky above. He lay flat upon the earth, burying his face in the dead leaves, trying to shut out the fearful brightness of the flashes of lightning. Cormac, whining and trembling, tried to creep ever closer, apparently sure that his master could protect him even from this terrible tumult that was so far outside the experience of either of them.

Then, all of a sudden, the storm was gone. The curtain of rain moved down the valley, passed the mouth of the Des Moines, and showed the wide, shining blue of the Mississippi. The deafening uproar overhead died away to distant growling and muttering, and the sweet, cool smell of wet willows came up to Dick as he sat amid the dripping trees.

His eyes were dazzled by the brilliance of the sunshine that came out in glory upon the wet world. It turned the green of the grass to emerald and the drops upon the leaves to diamonds. The whole valley was lit with an unearthly, a magical radiance;

so that it seemed there might be fairies hiding under every drenched bush; there might be elves and leprecauns swinging from the vines.

"You have an eye for fairy things," the little old woman had told him. And in this new country who could tell what he might not see?

In the stillness he could hear the rushing of the Des Moines and the deeper, steadier voice of the great river beyond. Then he and Cormac raised their heads together, caught to sudden attention by a new sound, the soft thudding of unshod hoofs upon the wet earth.

Down the hillside, through the trees and underbrush, without path or trail, came a slim, black horse at a headlong gallop. Upon his back was a lithe, dark-skinned rider, a boy of about Dick's own age, who swayed easily with the plunging motion of the horse, as though the two were one. His black hair was flying, his brown hand held a lance with a fluttering pennon of scarlet feathers, while from his arm swung a round shield of painted buffalo hide. Save for his copper skin, he might have been one of the Irish heroes out of Thomas Garrity's tales, an enchanted vision of the dim past.

The future was to make him Dick's comrade-in-arms and his beloved friend, but of this neither one nor the other could guess anything at that moment.

Unmindful of the boy and the dog who crouched in the brush, he went thundering past in his joyous, headlong race, and rode away into the flashing sunshine of the new, green world.

CHAPTER VIII

KATEQUA

IN the space of half an hour, Thomas Garrity set forth the plan that was to occupy them with many months of labor. There must be enough wild hay cut and cured to supply the sheep during the winter, there must be a stockade and a shed built to shelter the flock; then there must be a cabin for themselves. They staked out the shape and dimensions of the sheep's pen on the first day, and when Dick asked why the walls must be so thick and so stout, his comrade answered briefly—"Wolves!"

It was plain that if all this were to be accomplished before cold weather, there was no time to lose. Dick learned that a frontiersman must have skill at many things; so he set himself to learn as quickly as he could the proper sweep of a scythe and the most effective swing of an axe. To stand waist deep in the waving grass, that was now turning from green to yellow, to see the first light touch of autumn laid upon the hills, and to watch the gathering clouds of blackbirds darkening the sky overhead and flying so low that he could hear the swishing of their wings, all these gave him a strange thrill of pleasure that he could never have described. To go to bed at night with his muscles aching, but with the knowledge of a good day's work behind him, and with his mind full of the beauty and color and abundant life that he had been drinking in since morning—these were things to make him sleep deeper and wake more happily than ever in his life before.

One thing only became a source of anxiety and suspense. This was the strange, aloof attitude of the Indians. While day after day passed, they showed no signs of friendliness, no curiosity even, no hint that they had so much as observed the arrival of the strangers. What they were thinking, what their future action would be, neither Dick nor Thomas Garrity could attempt to guess.

It was not until the end of a week that Dick caught his second glimpse of the Indian boy. It was one hot, sunshiny morning, when Dick was cutting logs at the edge of the wood. Through the shafts of sunshine and shade, a slim, brown figure went by as silently as a shadow. This time the Indian was aware of the other's presence, for he flashed upon Dick a hasty, hostile glance as he strode past almost without turning his head. Dick, on his side, swung his axe and went on whistling his gay, Irish tune without missing a stroke or faltering on a note. A boy is quick to learn the customs of other boys; nor was Dick to be outdone in outward show of indifference.

Excitement ran tingling through him, however, for here was the real fulfillment of his dream; here was his first contact with the Indians. That quick, graceful lad was a person after all, and not a magic vision as Dick had almost been tempted to believe. He was real, but was he to be a friend or an enemy? Whichever he was, he would throw his whole heart into it, of that Dick felt sure. The memory of the lithe strength of that silently striding figure filled his mind for many days.

His first acquaintance with any of his unresponsive neighbors was to come about unexpectedly. Three days later, he had gone, at sunset, down to the river for water. His feet had already begun to mark a path down the bank and across a sandbar to where, by leaning over a stranded log, he could dip his pail into fairly deep water. As he came down the bank he noticed that there were footprints other than his own in the sand, and that some one was stooping over the log at the edge of the bar. He saw a black, bent head and a bare brown arm, and hoped for a moment that it was the Indian boy again. As the figure straightened up, however, he saw that it was a girl, slimmer and smaller than the boy he had seen, but not unlike him. She wore a straight dress of white deerskin, belted with beads, and had a band of brighter colored beads in her black, braided hair. For a moment she looked about her anxiously, as though seeking some way to reach the bank without meeting the stranger, but seeing that was impossible, she finally came slowly toward him across the sand.

She carried a big iron kettle, probably the great treasure of her household, since among these Indians vessels for carrying water are few and inadequate. Anything made of metal is a great prize; but this precious kettle, when once filled, was so heavy she could scarcely lift it. So evident was it that she would have difficulty in carrying it up the steep bank, that Dick ventured to take the ponderous thing from her.

She looked surprised at first, since such an offer of help was entirely unknown to Indian custom, then alarmed, lest his purpose should be to rob her of the treasured kettle. In a moment, however, she seemed to understand his intention, and yielded up the unwieldy burden. It was far heavier than he thought, so that, when he chanced to step upon a muddy spot on the steep path, he slipped, lost his balance, and rolled down the slope, followed by the rolling kettle. The girl regarded him gravely for a minute, then, as he sat up, grinning ruefully, she burst into peals of whole-hearted, friendly laughter.

Dick arose, laughing also, refilled the kettle and, this time, carried it safely up the bank. Since it seemed necessary to say something, even though they could not understand each other, he observed, as he put it upon the ground—

"I should like to carry it all the way home for you."

She looked at him solemnly and made some answer in her own tongue, quite as incomprehensible to him as his remark had been to her. Then she burst out into delighted laughter again, in which he joined. He began to feel that a joke in common will carry people further into friendship than hours of talk.

She sat down upon the green bank, motioned him to do likewise, and began to initiate him into the mysteries of that curious unshared skill of the Indians in talking by signs. With supple hands and shoulders, with expressive face and nodding head, she told him a world of things that no one would have guessed could be communicated other than by words. She made him understand that the water was growing shallow near the Indian village, so that she had come hither to fill her kettle where it was deeper and cooler. The lodge had not been there long, she told him, for the whole village had just come back from their journey westward for the summer hunting, and were now getting their dwellings ready for the winter, just as he and Thomas Garrity were doing. She lived in a lodge with her mother and a very old, wrinkled squaw, her grandmother. She had no father, but she had a brother, a glorious, brave brother, so her expression and gestures made clear. He and she looked a little alike, but he was taller and two years older.

Then, since Dick seemed to follow so well this odd, silent speech, she went on to talk to him about himself. She made him see his own arrival with Thomas Garrity, the coming and the departure of the three boats, her amazement and wonder at those unfamiliar animals, the sheep. She pictured the breaking of the storm and Dick's taking refuge with Cormac at the edge of the wood. It was evident that she must have been hiding in the brush somewhere near them at the time, for she described, with graphic movements of her brown hands, how the sun had come out after the rain, and how the Indian boy, unseeing, had ridden past them down the hill. That, she let him know with pride in her eyes, was her well-beloved brother.

She tried to tell him something further about that brother, something to do with the reason for his riding up the hill amid the rain and the crashing thunder. But here even Dick's ready wit could not follow, so she abandoned the effort to explain. But she had a question to ask. She acted out unmistakably the process of cutting and carrying away the hay. For what purpose, she wished to know did he and Thomas Garrity perform such labor?

And Dick, entering into the spirit of this strange conversation, made her understand that when the cold winter came (a succession of shivers made that clear), and when the snow was deep upon the ground (he held up his hand to show her exactly how deep), then the four-footed animals would eat it to keep from starving.

She answered with delighted laughter, for she had understood every one of his clumsy attempts at speaking by signs. Which of the animals ate the hay, she now inquired, was it the yellow-coated friend who ran always at his master's heels, and was so unlike the dogs of the Indian village, or was it that great creature with circling horns at each side of his head, and with his company of squaws and children? Ah, yes, she understood perfectly now. Cormac did not eat hay, it was only the sheep.

She stood up and spoke for the first time. "Katequa," she said, pointing to herself. It was evidently her name. Her brother's name, she made him understand, was Mateo.

Dick, in turn, told her his own name. "Dick Martin," she managed to repeat it, although it was plain the short, sharp syllables were very foreign to her rippling speech. Finally, taking up her kettle, she went away toward the village. The boy could hear her still struggling with his name as she went along, "Dick Martin—Dick Martin."

The acquaintance that had begun so well seemed for a time to be destined to go no further. Weeks passed without Dick's having a second meeting with Katequa. Once, as he was hunting along the crest of the bluff, he saw her walking through the woods with her brother and although she would have stopped to speak to Dick, Mateo hurried her on with a tug at her arm and a muttered command. Dick looked over his shoulder after they had passed and saw them both looking back, she with a friendly smile, he with that same look of wondering hostility. More than once, however, as he went out with his axe or his gun, he was certain that the faint rustling in the underbrush was not always made by a shy quail or a scuttling rabbit, and that Katequa's eyes, peering from behind trees or through the curtains of matted vines, were following him furtively wherever he went.

For a boy who had never before handled a gun, he was beginning to be an excellent hunter, and brought home every day quail or ducks or at best a brown rabbit to grace their dinner. So far, he and Thomas Garrity lived in a tent that had once been white but was now growing gray and weather-beaten and would before long, they hoped, be replaced by a more solid dwelling. They had cut and stored enough hay to tide their flock over the winter and had roofed over the great stack with a thatch of bark and of willow branches as protection from the rain and snow. The stockade for the sheep, with a rude shed in the most sheltered corner, had at last been finished, with walls high enough and strong enough to satisfy even Thomas Garrity. Now they were prying up big blocks of the soft limestone of the bluff and moving them into place as a foundation for the house. The necessary logs had been cut and rolled down the hill; but this portion of the work went slowly. The stones and the rough tree trunks were heavy; and, industrious as Thomas Garrity and Dick might be, they were only two workmen and no very skillful ones at that.

September had merged into a golden and glorious October, with days that were warm at noontide, but fresh and frosty at evening and morning. Across the slopes of the hills, close to the ground, had crept a crimson flood, as the sumac and the creeping woodbine turned from green to clear, flaming red. Then the autumn began to touch the trees, rising in a higher and higher tide of glowing color; the oaks showing bronze and russet and maroon; the maples every shade of scarlet and yellow. From day to day, almost from hour to hour, the change went on. The tent and the site of the cabin were on

KATEQUA   107

a slope that overlooked the two rivers and the
low-lying bars and islands where the streams met.
Every morning when Dick came out to begin his
work of the day he stood still for a moment on the
frost-tipped grass to see how the rush of color had
gone farther up the valley than the day before; how
the gold of the willows at the water's edge was
clearer and purer; and how the great Mississippi
rolled down its wide waters of deeper blue under
the glowing blue of the cloudless sky.

"It cannot last," he kept thinking; but day after
day passed in unbroken procession of untouched
splendor.

Streams of geese and ducks went by overhead,
traveling by day and night to accomplish their
journey southward; so that often, when he awoke
in the dark, Dick could hear their voices talking to
one another in the sky. Sometimes in the mornings
the sandbar below them would be white with a flock
of swans, stopping to preen themselves and to rest
a little. When they arose in circling flight, Dick
could watch them dip and swing and change in color,
gray when they were tilted against the sun, half
white, half dark, as they wheeled again, then silver-
white as they caught the full sunshine and sped
away in straight, swift passage. Dick kicked the
backlog of their spent and covered fire, and sniffed
the perfume of the blue, sweet woodsmoke that

curled up from the smoldering coals. He had never known that any one could be so happy.

He would fall to thinking of the Indians, and realized that they were close akin to these wild birds passing overhead. Life was sweet to them; it was also uncertain. It was made up entirely of a battle to keep alive, an endless struggle against varied enemies, with the result that anything strange to them must seem hostile and dangerous. Since they held their own lives cheap, they so considered the lives of others. If you were friends with them and were trusted by them, you were completely safe. But if they decided your presence was a danger, they would think nothing of putting an end to you, "leaving you in the brush with the painted feathers of an arrow between your ribs," as Anthony Robins had said. He would think of Anthony Robins, small, stingy, and meager, and laugh at the picture of how utterly out of place he would be in this hard-working, heart-filling, beautiful life.

Dick was setting forth one morning at the end of October with his rifle on his shoulder. Thomas Garrity, having taught him to shoot, now left to him the task of replenishing the larder, and was busy squaring the logs that had been piled ready to build their cabin. Dick was still in the open, climbing the lower slope of the hillside, when the Indian girl came running out of the woods to meet him.

It gave him a strange start to hear her speak his name—"Dick Martin." He smiled a delighted greeting.

She, however, forebore to smile, but immediately began telling him some elaborate tale by means of signs. She pointed to the big river, made a rocking movement with her hands and held up two fingers— she must mean two canoes. He looked down toward the smooth blue of the river, saw nothing, and looked back again, puzzled. She was more earnest now; she depicted the overturning of the canoes, and men swimming to the shore. He turned quickly to the river again, thinking that she meant some one was in danger, and that he must go to the rescue. But she motioned him to stay. No, she managed to reassure him, no one had need of him. She went on more and more eagerly, but he had lost the thread of her meaning, and could only stare at her in bewilderment. At the end she pointed to the tent near which Thomas Garrity was visible with his axe, she pointed to Dick himself, put her finger on her lips as though to denote silence and caution, then made the motions of lifting and carrying a burden, and waved her hand toward the woods. He shook his head in mute confession that he did not understand.

Her face grew more troubled as she sat down upon a log and very slowly and carefully went through the whole pantomime again. It seemed, so he vaguely realized, that she wished him and Thomas Garrity to take refuge in the woods from some danger which she was trying in vain to describe. As his blank look still made plain that he did not understand, she got up and, with hanging head, walked slowly back into the forest. At the edge of the wood her brother met her, and the two talked earnestly together, but only for a moment. It seemed as though she were urging him to try to make things clear where she had failed, but he only sent Dick a lowering look, turned on his heel in curt refusal, and disappeared among the trees. With dragging footsteps she followed him, never looking back.

For a short space Dick stood pondering, then shouldered his rifle and went on.

"I will tell Thomas Garrity about it, and see if he understands," he thought, "but there will be time enough when I have hunted across the hill."

An hour later he came out of the wood again, so proud and excited with the bringing down of his first wild turkey, that he had scarcely any memory of his interview with the Indian girl. The big bird with its feathers ruffled and its bronze wings extended, hung over his shoulder, a prize indeed to fall to the rifle of so inexperienced a woodsman. He could hardly wait to show it to Thomas Garrity.

KATEQUA

He ran quickly down the slope, then stopped, transfixed with surprise. Two canoes were drawn up on the sandbar and three men were walking in single file up the path toward the hillside where the tent was pitched. He noticed, as he came near, that all three of them had faces so darkened by much sunburn and by little washing, as almost to conceal the fact that they were white men. They all wore buckskin shirts and heavy boots, and each had a hunting knife at his belt and a rifle on his shoulder. Dick had seen men like them at St. Louis, and knew them to be a company of trappers and traders with the Indians on their journey northward for the winter season. As he looked into the shifting black eyes of the man who came first up the hill he had an instant of misgiving, which was, however, lost immediately in his delight at the thought of visitors of their own kind in the lonely valley.

"We're just in time for dinner, I see," the man greeted him. The second trapper coming up behind him grinned broadly and spoke in an accent that marked him as a Frenchman. "Ah, what good fortune, a turkey! And we as hungry as wolves!"

Cormac came to sniff at the heels of the newcomers and, to Dick's surprise, growled inhospitably at the first. With the second man he seemed puzzled, growling first and then wagging his tail, as though uncertain whether to think well or ill of him. Toward the third he showed such furious dislike that he had to be sent away to stay with the sheep. Even Thomas Garrity showed less pleasure than Dick in the arrival of the strangers, but he greeted them with grave welcome and helped to spread a feast for them of beans and bacon, the savory turkey, and the flapjacks that did duty for bread. The guests did, indeed, eat like wolves and one of them never spoke until the long meal was at an end.

The most talkative member of the party, whose name was Melrose, so he said, plied Dick with questions, and led him on to tell much of his work and of the life he and Thomas Garrity were leading.

"Have you had trouble with the Indians yet? Do you know how big their village is?" the man wished to know.

So far there had been no trouble, although they had felt it best to keep away from the encampment, Dick told him. He had looked down on the village from the hill; it held about fifteen lodges and had a great herd of horses that grazed on the meadow near by.

"They're a village of the Sac-and-Fox tribe," the stranger said. "We had a brush last year with another lot of the same Indians that live farther north, on the Rock River. That band has made up its mind that no white men shall settle near them, but these, it seems, haven't decided yet. They are rich, are they? Indians measure their riches by the number of horses they own, and you say these have a great many? They'll be raided by the Sioux from the north if they aren't careful. The Sioux and the Sac-and-Foxes are old enemies."

Thomas Garrity spoke, almost for the first time during the meal.

"You are going into the Sioux country?" he said.

"Yes, we go every winter to trap and buy furs and trade with the Indians, and come back in the spring after the ice goes out. We've taught the red demons that we'll take no nonsense from them, so we do pretty well. You are getting ready for the cold weather, I see."

"We have still to build our cabin," Thomas Garrity replied briefly.

"But you have a good lot of supplies? You brought in plenty from St. Louis to last you until spring?"

"Enough," conceded Thomas Garrity, "but no more than that."

Melrose frowned and turned to Dick. "That's your storage tent, I suppose, behind the other? And you have a good deal put away there?"

Dick assured him eagerly that they were comfortably supplied, and so far, had shot so much game that they had scarcely touched their pork and bacon.

The third member of the company, a burly man with a dull face and a heavy neck like a bull's, grunted when he heard this statement. Dick looked up and saw that Thomas Garrity's eyes were fixed upon his own; but he could not understand what his comrade's strange expression could mean.

"And powder and shot," pursued Melrose, "have you plenty of that?"

Yes, Dick assured him, Thomas Garrity had been wise enough to purchase a good stock of ammunition that would last easily until spring.

"Good," replied the other, "good." And the burly man grunted again.

They had all finished eating now, and the second man, he who spoke like a Frenchman and whom the other addressed as Gil Surette, pulled out his pipe. He was the one about whom Cormac had seemed so puzzled.

"We have need of tobacco," he announced.

Without answering, Thomas Garrity brought out a leather bag of tobacco, which passed from hand to hand, as the men filled their pipes. Dick noticed that the last man, who had nearly emptied it, put the bag into his pocket, but that Thomas Garrity made no comment.

"M'sieur, we have had a great misfortune." It

was the Frenchman who went on with the talk, while the first lapsed into silence. It was as if he had played his part, and the other, obviously the leader, now took the matter in hand. "Yesterday one of our canoes overset in the swift current and, while we struggled to save what was in it, the other went over also. We got out our traps and guns, but all else, powder, food for the winter, everything, was gone."

"You have had bad luck," returned Thomas Garrity. "You will have to go back to St. Louis for more. I can give you enough food to supply you on the way. We have not a great deal, but we will spare you what we can."

There was a long silence before any one answered. Dick suddenly felt his heart knock against his ribs. There was danger from these men, the danger of which Katequa had tried to warn him. Something was about to happen. What it was, he did not yet understand. But, in that dreadful stillness, it came to him suddenly that he had talked too much, that Thomas Garrity had tried to silence him, but had not been able. The Frenchman spoke at last very gently, his quick utterance dropping almost to a drawl.

"It will not be as you think, M'sieur. It is you and the boy who will go back to St. Louis, while we take what you have here and go on. We cannot delay our season's trapping; we would lose much and valuable time should we go back. We of the frontier have learned to lay hands on what we need. As the boy has told my friend Melrose, you have much put by for the winter. That is lucky. We can give you enough to get to St. Louis before you starve. It is a thousand pities you have no canoe and must walk."

His sharp teeth showed as he smiled his odd, wolfish smile. The silence was so tense that no one even moved. The fire crackled and the noise of the rushing river came up to them from below, but otherwise there was not a sound.

"I know what you are thinking, M'sieur," the Frenchman went on at last, "but we are three men, very strong men, and you are but one man, no longer very young, and a boy not yet very old. You have suspected us a little, but not enough. Observe that you have done what a frontiersman should never do. You have permitted a stranger to get between you and your gun."

It was true. Dick sat nearest the tent door and Thomas Garrity next the fire, while the three strangers had edged themselves between.

"What use of resistance?" continued the drawl of the French trapper. "You try to fight us and we make an end of you both, with little trouble. No one will know! And should any person chance to come later and find you dead, it is easy to think that the Indians did it."

The man named Melrose broke in, "There was an Indian boy circling round your camp as we came up the hill. I never saw such an unfriendly face. If there is any question of who shot you, he is the one to lay it on. So we'll just take your bacon and flour and powder and go along. We might slaughter a sheep or two, besides. Wild turkey is good, but mutton would taste better."

The big, burly man spoke for the first time.

"Look at that great ram over yonder. I'd like to taste his ribs, broiled over the coals. They'd be more tender than mountain sheep—eh, boys?"

Dick had never felt such rage as took possession of him at that moment. To rob them in return for their hospitality! To consider fastening the crime of murder upon Mateo, who, though he had never been a friend, had at least been an honorable enemy, and to hear that great, thick-necked glutton smacking his lips over the prospect of feasting on the ram! His ram!

He snatched up his rifle and stood at the opening of the tent.

"It is you who are mistaken. You—you'll not have anything of ours," he cried, choking with fury.

The tall Frenchman jumped to his feet with the easy nimbleness of some wild creature of the woods. Even the heavy, silent man had moved with amazing quickness, had grasped the gun beside him, and held it leveled at Thomas Garrity.

"Watch the old one and leave the young wildcat to me," the Frenchman ordered in a quick undertone. "Do you recollect, young sir," he said to Dick, returning to his gentle drawl, "that your gun is loaded for wild turkey, and you are thinking it will stop three men? Men of the woods, as we are, could hold a dozen of your little bullets, and never be the wiser. It is best to do this with your small gun."

With one sweep of his long arm he knocked the rifle from Dick's hand, so that it went spinning away into the bushes. It went off as it fell; and the report brought Cormac dashing up the slope from where he had been watching the sheep. He made a leaping snap at the Frenchman's shoulder, and came away with a mouthful of torn buckskin. The man turned on him with a curse and drew his knife.

"Back, Cormac, down," cried Dick. The dog would be killed he knew, should he get within striking distance of that sharp blade.

The Frenchman strode nearer. "Will you give me what I want?" he demanded.

"No," cried Dick.

He felt that his heart would break with helpless fury, but, unarmed as he was, he still stood his ground.

CHAPTER IX

WILD HONEY

THE tall Frenchman turned round upon his companions. A change came over his dark face, a change that Dick could not understand. He stood, tense, wondering, waiting for what the man was to do next.

Cormac, ordered back from his headlong attack, was sitting very tall and straight upon the grass, his head up, his ears at attention, the white ruff standing out around his neck. To Dick's amazement, his tail suddenly began to move gayly and his ears to drop.

Very slowly the Frenchman laid his knife upon the grass and held up his hand a few feet from the ground.

"So high," he exclaimed, "so high he is, not up to my tall shoulder, and with no weapon, yet there he stands, ready to tear me to pieces should I touch his bacon or his bullets or his precious dog! We have faced danger in the forests and thought ourselves brave, but he is braver, is it not so?"

Cormac's tail wagged openly. He had been the first to note the change in the man's expression and understood now, from his altered voice, that the danger was over.

"We cannot rob you, M'sieur," the French trapper said to Thomas Garrity, a tinge of regret in his tone. "You have faced death without fear and your young comrade here has defied us all. We men of the woods have our own laws, we must respect those who are bolder than we."

The two others laid down their guns without a word, although the biggest man looked at the fat sheep grazing nearest him and sighed deeply. Gil Surette held out a long, sinewy hand to Dick, which the boy took after a moment's distrustful hesitation. He was too dazed to realize yet just what had happened. The French trapper sat down easily upon a log and resumed his talk with Thomas Garrity.

"You offered one plan," he began, "and I proposed another. Now we will consider a third. We, the three of us, are going on a long, long, journey into the north. Should we all return to St. Louis for new supplies, we would lose so much time that we would miss setting our traps with the first snow. We would find that the Indians have arranged to dispose of their furs elsewhere than to us. It would take time, and perhaps some harshness, to persuade them to do otherwise. It would have been so simple to take your flour and bacon, since it seemed we needed them worse than you. But you are not the sort that a man can willingly rob and leave to starve."

"Thank you," returned Thomas Garrity, drily. "Your compliments are of a sort we are not used to. And what is this new plan of yours?"

"It is that I send Melrose forward on the northern journey alone, you giving him sufficient supplies to keep him from starving during the first cold month. My other comrade and I will go back to St. Louis, load our canoe with new stores, make good with you what Melrose has taken, and follow him into the north woods. He will have begun the season's trapping and we will arrive in time to continue it."

He smiled broadly as he looked from Thomas Garrity to Dick.

"It is true you may think that you will never see us again, and that our promises mean nothing. It is a risk you will run, but bold men are willing to face some odds. What say you, my friends?"

"I agree," declared Thomas Garrity promptly.

These men were fierce, lawless, cruel when there seemed to be the need of it; but it was plain that they were genuine. Whether they promised to rob or to restore, they would keep their word.

"And my young enemy here, does he agree also,

or will he shoot me through, with his popgun, the moment I lay a finger on his stores?" the Frenchman pursued.

"Yes. I am willing, too," Dick answered. He tried to speak with dignity; but in spite of himself his serious face widened to a smile. The tall woodsman laughed gayly in return.

"Now is everything pleasant again," he observed cheerfully. "And since it is so, suppose we three bend our backs to helping you for a little with that cabin you are preparing to build. Those logs are of a great thickness for two to lift alone, and you also have need of haste to be ready for the cold winter."

It was wonderful what five could accomplish, working where only two had toiled before. The foundation stones were pried up and leveled, the big logs rolled into place and piled one upon the other. The work went forward with gay talk and shouts of laughter; so that it seemed the last thing possible that these fellow laborers had been threatening each other's lives an hour or two before.

One small mishap, only, disturbed the peaceful toil of the sunny afternoon. The bull-necked man —his unsuitable name proved to be Ebenezer Wren —was no lover of hard work. Although he could lift twice the weight that any of the others could, he was not so eager as they to labor. He had contrived to slip away from the scene of the house-building and was poking about the camp fire, hoping, probably, to find some remains of the midday feast upon which to indulge his never failing appetite. He did not observe that the big ram had grazed closer and closer and now stood observing his movements with lively interest. The burly Ebenezer had finally come across the carcass of the turkey with its bones not quite picked bare. With broadly beaming countenance he pulled off a drumstick, seated himself comfortably on a log and, holding the morsel in both hands, took one large, delicious bite.

He had no chance for a second one. The broad, stooping back was too tempting a mark for the ram. Cormac must have seen him back away, settle his feet, and lower his horns for a charge. Cormac might even have headed him off in his furious rush, but the undutiful sheep dog did no such thing. He sat before the tent with his tongue out and his tail wagging and made no move. Bang—came the impact of the great horns against the wide back, and over went the feasting idler with the sickening gasp of one whose breath is knocked completely out of his body.

He got up, his hair full of ashes, his face red with rage, and his big hand at the hunting knife in his belt.

"I'll cut the black heart out of him," he roared with a string of oaths. But Surette, with two long strides, was at his side, tapping him quickly on the shoulder.

"You will go back to your work and leave the wise beast in peace," he ordered. "You have been overtaken by the usual fate of idlers."

And the big man, without further words, returned to his task and accomplished prodigies of toil before the darkness put an end to their labor.

The next morning Melrose set out northward; but the other two maintained that they could still spare a day, and once more helped Dick and Thomas Garrity to rear the walls of their dwelling. Even the roofbeams were in place by evening, to such good purpose had been the toil of the quick Frenchman and the burly giant. And at sunrise of the morning after, these two also put their canoe into the water and paddled away southward. Dick, standing on the hillside and waving a gay good-by, watched them as they launched out into the big Mississippi and dwindled away to a black speck against the blue.

Thomas Garrity at the time of their going said little of the adventure and nothing at all, for a time, of Dick's ever ready tongue which had wrought such trouble, or of his brave stand after the mischief was made. As he filled his pipe by the fire that evening, he made his first comment on the subject.

"The trappers hate the settlers," he declared, "for

their coming means filling up the country, driving out the game, and putting an end to fur trade in that region. Therefore, they resent the spreading of the settlements as bitterly as do the Indians. But they may as well attempt to hold back the waters of the Mississippi!"

Dick stirred the fire, so that the red flames leaped, and moved to closer to it, for the nights were growing cold.

"They are strange men, these trappers," Thomas Garrity went on. "They love their hard, dangerous life, and come to it from every rank and station. That Frenchman has been a man of honor and education; so one can judge from his speech, the only mark of a different life that he could not leave behind him. He was born, perhaps, in some great and noble house; he will die, starved or shot, alone in the woods. What adventures he will have seen first, what strange things he will have done!"

"Do you think he would have robbed us—that he would have killed us?" asked Dick.

"Surely, had his need been more pressing. He has struggled so fiercely for existence against cold and hunger, wild beasts and Indians, that he knows no law but his own need. Yet, there are fine things still left in him. And how easily he ruled the others, just by his greater strength of spirit! I do not know whether to be more surprised that he wished

WILD HONEY

to rob us, or that he forbore to do so. We were as tempting prey as one of the ducks we hear quacking overhead would be to a wild red hawk."

"We had warning," Dick told him ruefully, "the Indian girl tried to tell me they were coming, and that we should hide our stores from them. She even knew we should not tell them too much about what we had. But I could not understand. I could not even be quiet when you wanted me to be. It was my fault. I nearly lost us everything. How could I have sat there like a chattering fool and told all our secrets."

"If you nearly lost us everything, you were also the means of saving us," returned Thomas Garrity. "You do not often say too much; it was only that you were starved for talk with white men like ourselves. The girl, Katequa, tried to warn us, do you say? I wonder how she could have known of their coming. Well, well, it is a past adventure now, and we will think of it no more. Stir up the fire again, and I will tell you the story of Fergus mac Roy mac Rury and how he overthrew his enemies."

When the story was finished and the fire had died down and Dick had crawled into his cedar-bough bed, he thought once more of Katequa and her message. How, indeed, had she come to know of the men and the upsetting of their canoes? Was it her brother who had seen it, and who had sent her to give warning? Could it have been? He fell asleep still wondering.

He had no chance to tell Katequa of what had happened, for he caught not even a glimpse of her for some time. He did, however, see her brother for a moment that was to live long in his memory.

Dick chanced to be walking at the summit of the bluff that overlooked the Mississippi, tramping along through the red blackberry vines and the scarlet sumac. He looked down and observed a hollow in the face of the slope, a warm, grassy niche where the sun lay nearly all day and whence one could look out over miles of blue river, even as far as the ruffled waters of the great rapids far above. Here was sitting Mateo, with his chin in his hand and his elbows on his knees, staring out over the river, and so absorbed that he seemed to regard nothing else in the world. To Dick's surprise he had a comrade, evidently a well-known one. Cormac was sitting close by him with his long, yellow head laid across the Indian boy's brown knees. For a second Dick felt a pang of jealousy that his dog should be showing allegiance to another, but it was a feeling that passed as quickly as it came.

There was something unbelievably sad in Mateo's intent face as he gazed out on that wide, blue flood, which he seemed to love with the intense devotion

WILD HONEY 129

of his whole being. Better than long hours of talk could have told him, Dick understood at that moment the feeling that an Indian bears for his home and his hunting ground, for the hills and meadows and rivers in which his free life moves.

Cormac, feeling his master's presence, looked up and wagged his tail. Instantly the Indian was on his feet and had vanished down the slope with the speed and silence of a passing gust of wind.

The work on the cabin had been carried so far that the rough little house afforded more certain shelter now than did the tent. There was much to be done still—the logs to be chinked with clay, the bark roof to be made more permanent, the temporary fireplace of four big stones to be built into a chimney.

"But it will serve us," Thomas Garrity said, "and now we have a home at last. I wish——" He stood on the doorstone and looked out across the river, stood there so long in silence that Dick was obliged to ask—

"What is it you wish?"

"We have a roof over our heads, and stout walls to keep the wind away, we have food and flocks and all the lands we want, and the greatest and finest river in the country rolling past our dwelling. So, in the fashion of all men who have the whole of what they need, I must needs wish for one thing more—

a little thing—a horseshoe to nail over the door. It would be more like home had we some such foolish charm to keep the bad luck away."

"But the Indian horses do not wear shoes," Dick objected practically. "How could we get one?"

"We cannot," replied Thomas Garrity easily, "but a man must always wish for something it is impossible to have. Better a small thing like a horseshoe, than the moon!"

As they sat through the first long evening before the blaze between the firestones, Dick's mind kept going back to those little thatched cottages in Ireland where each one had some such charm to drive away ill fortune, or to bring the good will of the Little People. Suppose Bridget Anne were sitting there with her knitting beside the fire. With her knowledge of fairy lore, what would she say must be done to bring good fortune to the new house? She would set out a bowl of cream, he was certain, with a pot of cheese or of new butter, so that the fairies would be friendly.

Dick took up a wooden bowl and began going to and fro among the piles of stores that had not yet been put in order. He gathered up a handful of bright-colored beans and, from a bag of greatly treasured apples, he took one of the largest and reddest. Then he cracked a quantity of the round, white hickory nuts and rich, sweet pecans that he had gathered in the woods. With these he filled the bowl heaping full.

"What are you doing?" Thomas Garrity asked.

"I am going to put this outside," Dick answered, "just—just to see what it will bring in a new country." Thomas Garrity smiled broadly and offered neither approval nor objection.

The night was cloudy, with a high, warm wind and a promise of rain. Dick set down the bowl at the edge of the doorstone, went in quickly, and closed the door.

The threatened showers came in the night, pattering flurries of autumn rain. Dick, awaking for a moment, heard it upon the bark roof and thought how different it sounded from the noise of rain splashing against the flimsy canvas walls of a tent. It was such a homelike, comfortable sound that it lulled him quickly to sleep again.

In the morning he hastened out to see what his bowl had brought. In the soft, wet earth about the doorstep were various woodland footprints: a rabbit had come up to sniff and nibble at the apple; three squirrels had ventured near to investigate the nuts; and an inquisitive crow had left abundant crooked tracks when he had come to carry away the beans. Thomas Garrity spoke from the doorway behind him.

"Do you see anywhere the footprints of your

great-great-grandfather's friend, the little green man?"

Dick straightened up from his examination of the record of the night's visitors. "No," he admitted cheerfully, "he has not found us yet. Perhaps he will come to-night, or maybe he will wait a little longer. Bridget Anne used to say that fairies often waited until the seventh night, to make the luck quite sure."

Evening after evening Dick, rather shamefacedly, put out his wooden bowl with its friendly offering. It was always rifled in the morning, for boldly inquisitive creatures came down from the woods to see what he had to give them. Everything, from little deermice up to the clumsy feet of a porcupine, left traces about the doorstep. It was not possible to spare more from their supplies brought for the winter, but there were always nuts and berries and the round, red fruit of wild hawthorn.

It was on the seventh night that he came out to feel a chill wind and to see rolling gray clouds scudding across the sky, with only a sprinkle of stars on the far horizon.

"We should have a visit from the green man to-night," he told Thomas Garrity with laughing confidence, "so I must put out the best I have to give."

"And will he bring you the luck he brought your great-great-grandfather, I wonder?" questioned

Thomas Garrity, with a chuckle. "There is one thing that we can be sure will come to-night, and that is snow."

He was right. Dick opened the door in the morning to a white world, although the snow had come so softly in the darkness that he had not heard it. The sky was gray and the flaming woods had grown dull and brown. A rising wind was beginning to strip the branches and whirl the flying leaves across the hill.

Upon the doorstone stood the bowl. It had been emptied and filled again, for within it, instead of nuts, was a piece of clean bark bearing a square of wild honey. There were footprints in the snow, not of rabbit or squirrel, but of moccasined feet. Could they be Katequa's, Dick wondered for a moment. But no, they were larger than hers would be, and measured a longer stride. It was Mateo who had come at last to make offers of friendship.

CHAPTER X

COMPANION OF THE THUNDER

THE light snowfall had not really marked the beginning of winter, but only the change from the bright hues of October to the still peace of Indian summer. For a few days the leaves dropped like rain on every side, leaving the twigs outlined, intricate and graceful, against a blue, cloudless sky. The world was clothed no longer in scarlet and gold, but in a soft, sunny haze; the nights were colder; the morning frost was whiter on the grass; but the days were mild and bright and still.

"I wonder if Gil Surette is coming back to us," Dick observed more than once as the time passed. Enough days had elapsed for the journey to St. Louis and back again to have been made with ease.

"I am sure he will come," Thomas Garrity always answered. "He is a man who would keep his word, either for good or for evil."

It was during these days of shining, peaceful weather that Dick's acquaintance with the Indian boy and girl, after being so long delayed, blossomed

COMPANION OF THE THUNDER 135

into open friendliness. Katequa and Mateo came again with a gift for the wooden bowl; they met Dick on the doorstone, and after a moment of awkward shyness, fell to talking with him by means of signs. It was dried buffalo meat that they had brought; and they gave him an account, mostly through Katequa's means, of how the buffalo had been hunted on the prairies far to the westward, how the great beast had been brought down, and how the meat had been cut up and dried in the sun.

After that, the barriers of hostility and reserve were broken down and friendship came with a rush. The two boys met daily; they hunted together; they walked together along the crest of the bluff at twilight or, on afternoons that chanced to be free from their respective tasks, they sat in the sunny niche on the face of the hillside and talked without ceasing. Katequa's work was so different from theirs that she was not always able to join them; but whether she was present or not, there was always endless conversation.

How did they talk? At first it was by signs, but this did not last long. They were all so brimming with thoughts that they wished to share with one another, that they could not long be held to such a slow and clumsy method of exchanging ideas. They began to teach each other their different languages, so that in the end their talk was in a fantastic tongue of their very own, partly Indian, partly Gaelic, and partly English.

Dick heard now what was the errand that had carried Mateo to the top of the hill, that day of the storm when the Irish boy had first seen the Indian. Katequa told him of it one day when her brother chanced to be absent. She explained that Mateo had always been fascinated by the terrifying glory of a thunderstorm, and could never be persuaded to bide safely in the lodge when the thunder-god was rolling his great voice along the bluffs. Among some tribes the warriors went out with drums and eagle-bone whistles, with arrows and guns and lances to threaten and drive away the storm clouds. But Katequa's and Mateo's father, who was now dead, had always told them that the thunder-god brought the much-needed summer rains and was a friend and not an enemy. Without him the grass grew thin and dry, until there was no grazing for horses, or for the antelope and buffalo.

It was true that the god's long, shining arrows had sometimes demolished lodges and killed horses on the meadows, and had even, so it was said, destroyed a Sac-and-Fox chief, long ago. That made him a god to be feared and reverenced, so that it was only a true brave who could call him friend. When the thunder-god's great voice sounded in the

COMPANION OF THE THUNDER 137

sky, Mateo loved to ride to the hilltop, bearing his dead father's weapons of war, to shout greeting to the god as one warrior hails another.

Her brother was not old enough to be a real warrior yet, the girl told Dick, but already he went, in the tribe, by the nickname Companion of the Thunder. After he had been in his first battle with their enemies, the Sioux, and was made a true fighting-man, that would be his title. Had he been older when their father died, he would have been leader of the tribe, for their father was a great chief and it was fitting that his son should follow him. As it was, another man, Haidan, was head of the village, a good leader, but, "oh, not like our father," Katequa said.

To a dull or unpracticed eye, all Indians may seem to be alike, although they really vary quite as much as white people. Katequa and her brother resembled each other in many things, in their voices, in their erect bearing, in their eager and valiant spirits. He, however, was grave where she was always brimming with laughter; he was visionary where she was practical, even to a greater degree than others of her race. It had been a great trial to her to see Dick and Thomas Garrity preparing for the cold weather, and to be unable to tell them that they must add dried berries and fruits to their store, or sickness would overtake them before the winter was over. She showed Dick where to dig for wild carrots and how to slice and cure venison.

She and Mateo took him fishing in their canoe, and she taught him how to dry the fish in the smoke of the fire. Dick felt like an awkward giant the first time he embarked in the light, easily swaying craft; and, in his clumsy attempts at learning to paddle, he upset them twice into the cold current of the Des Moines. None of them, however, minded a ducking, even in November; and in the end he learned to paddle almost as skillfully as they. There was one glorious day when they took him on a long expedition beyond the low islands at the mouth of the Des Moines, and up against the current of the big river as far as those rapids that Dick used to hear roaring in the night.

They found famous fishing below the riffles, among the reefs with the white water tumbling over them, so that they came home with the canoe heavily laden and with Dick's muscles aching, but with a great satisfaction in his heart. Such a day, such sport, such friends! He, Katequa, and Mateo seemed to have been at one with one another and with the great, blue river, the softly singing winds, and the cloudless sky.

It was not until the third week of their friendship that the brother and sister took him for his first visit to the Indian village. Dick had often

COMPANION OF THE THUNDER 139

looked down upon it as he hunted across the hills, and had observed how the lodges were set up in a wide circle and how a great herd of horses grazed upon the meadow by the river. He had not known that the lodge-poles were covered with tightly stretched buffalo hides, and that these were painted with gay pictures of deer, of beaver, of hunting scenes, and war parties. Some of the colors were old and faded; but many were new and resplendent with scarlet and ochre and orange yellow. Before each door stood the lance of the warrior to whom the lodge belonged, and beside it hung his shield. These also were gayly painted and hung with fan-shaped ornaments of dyed feathers that swung in the breeze. Everywhere was color, movement, and laughter, the gay voices of children, the cheerful speech of their elders, and the comfortable crackling of fires.

In Mateo's lodge, Dick was presented to the mother of his two friends, a thin, handsome woman, and to their grandmother, a wrinkled old squaw as dry and withered as a dead sycamore leaf. She set before him a wooden bowl of soup made of buffalo meat thickened with corn meal, and she smiled a wide, toothless smile when, by means of the few Indian words he had learned, he made her understand how good he thought it. Presently, while he was still eating, she nodded and pointed to the door to call his attention to an odd and gaudily dressed figure that had twice passed before the lodge.

It was an Indian woman, rather short in stature and thickset, decked out in all the finery that a savage wardrobe could possibly boast. Her dress of soft deerskin had fringes of elk's teeth and dangling strings of beads, and was stiff with embroidery of bright porcupine quills. Elaborate hoops and ornaments of beads hung from her ears. She wore an unwieldy necklace of grizzly bear's claws, while dangling from it was an ornament that was evidently her most treasured jewel, an iron horseshoe. Elk's teeth and bear's claws could be won by mere risk of life; beads and porcupine-quill embroidery were the fruit of patient labor; but a horseshoe must be picked up by chance near some white settlement, must shift from hand to hand, always increasing in value, and could finally be purchased only for the sum of three horses. Dick eyed the treasure wistfully, remembering Thomas Garrity's vain desire, but he dared not even speak to the magnificent lady.

She was the wife of the chief, so Katequa told him, and she dwelt in the big, new lodge at the center of the village. The old grandmother, given to gossiping even though she must converse almost entirely by signs, gave Dick to understand that the woman's husband owned a string of at least a hundred horses and that he denied his wife nothing.

The wrinkled squaw would have gone on endlessly, had not Mateo led Dick away to see the horses. As they walked through the village, Cormac followed at their heels, regarded with distant respect by the ragged Indian dogs. Dull-eyed creatures these were, showing no signs of intelligence or friendliness, and so nearly like wolves that they did not even know how to bark, but could only howl.

Beside the chief's dwelling was the largest wigwam of all, painted all over with awkward, but strangely real, figures of Indians and horses. This was the medicine lodge, Mateo told Dick, the place of meetings and councils and of the ceremonies that must be gone through before a war party could set out. The pictures, he explained, were of a certain battle with the Sioux, in which the Sac-and-Fox tribe had won a great victory.

"But their tribes have grown greater as ours have grown fewer and smaller," he concluded regretfully, "so we do not defeat them now. They are our worst enemies, the Sioux. The buffalo have disappeared from the shores of these rivers, so every summer we travel westward to hunt near the Mississippi's great, muddy brother, the Missouri, or even to pass beyond it. If we did not have the dried buffalo meat for the winter we could scarcely live."

"And do you make that long journey every year?" asked Dick.

"Every year when the spring comes," returned Mateo. "But the Sioux claim that western land as their hunting ground and always seek to drive us back from it. They try also to rob us of our horses, since we are rich in horses and they are very jealous. They know that without our ponies trained to hunt the buffalo, we could not get our supply of meat, so they are always hoping to ruin us by driving away or destroying our herd."

For a village of that size, the band of horses was indeed a great one. Several hundred rough-haired ponies with long manes and tumbled forelocks were cropping the dry grass of the meadows. Wiry, restless, bright-eyed animals they were and of all colors, black, white, sorrel, with a great number of those piebald ponies that Indians so greatly love. They were shy and suspicious of strangers, so that only a few of them would allow Dick to come near or to touch them.

Before leaving the lodge, Mateo had picked up two of the rude bridles that his tribe was wont to use, mere strips of rawhide that were knotted about the horse's lower jaw. With a quick motion he caught a grazing white pony by the forelock, led him up to Dick, and showed his friend how to slip the bridle into place. The horse belonged to Mateo's own string, three fleet buffalo horses, and five more who carried lodge-poles and bore the women

COMPANION OF THE THUNDER 143

of his family when the tribe moved. Although the greatest number belonged to the chief, the best horse, the leader of the herd, was Mateo's. This was the quick, black pony that he was riding on the day when Dick first saw him sweeping down the hill. The father of the black horse had belonged to Mateo's father, that special strain of fleet horses being always the property of the chief. Even though another man was now head of the village, the black leader of the herd was still Mateo's by right of his being son and heir to the bravest chief the tribe had ever had.

The black horse did not suffer himself to be caught as easily as the white one, but wheeled and shied and kicked up his heels when his master approached. This was more a matter of gay spirits than of real objection to being ridden, for he allowed himself to be bridled and mounted at last. Dick, after watching Mateo's easy swing as he caught the black mane and vaulted upon the horse's back, made a manful attempt to mount his own steed in the same fashion. It was a clumsy, scrambling effort, but it succeeded finally, and he found himself surprisingly at ease as his willing mount galloped away across the meadow. He had never known such delicious motion as the long, smooth lope of the wiry little beast who was doing his utmost to overtake his black companion. The two boys wheeled and circled; they raced and shouted; and finally, leaving the bottom lands by the river, they climbed the steep trail through the woods and came out upon the flat prairie lands above.

Near the Mississippi and the Des Moines the bluffs and hillsides were cut into steep, rough valleys by the smaller tributary streams. Once beyond these small creeks and watercourses, Dick could see the level lands roll away to the horizon, unbroken by hill or tree or dwelling of mankind. The long, dry grass, standing in some places as high as the ponies' backs, was trodden into crooked trails by deer and horses, trails which covered the whole plain with myriad windings. Where it was still thick and tall, a thousand small rustlings told where partridges sheltered or rabbits hid, small, white-tailed bundles of fur which went bouncing away almost under the ponies' feet. Swift shadows of clouds went drifting across the wide prairie, so that now the boys were in shade, now they were shouting and galloping in the sun.

Mateo showed him how to put both hands at the sides of his mouth and to send forth a long, echoing cry. "It is so we shout when we ride to war," he said.

It was late when they returned, with the horses tired and the sun almost gone. They dipped down into the valley and came out once more upon the

COMPANION OF THE THUNDER 145

meadow where the grass was greener and sounded soft under the horses' feet. Here and there they rustled through tiny patches of abandoned garden plots where pumpkins had grown, or beans, or where some dried stalks of corn still stood upright. Here, so Mateo told him, the women dug laboriously in the early spring, planted a handful of beans or grain or melon seed, and left the young sprouting things to shift for themselves while the tribe was away for the summer hunting. Plants grew lustily in the rich, black soil, so that, if no deer trampled them or nibbled the tender tops, if no muskrats burrowed in the soft earth, the little gardens flourished greatly and yielded succulent harvests for the Indians' homecoming. After the unvaried fare of fresh buffalo meat all summer, the juicy fruits of the garden seemed so good that they were apt to be consumed in the course of a few days, with little left to be dried and stored for the winter. The Indians, as Dick was to learn, had small thought for the future, beyond the putting aside of enough food to keep themselves from the danger of actual starvation. They feasted when there was plenty; they endured dire want without complaint; and even after the most bitterly hungry winters, they showed no greater foresight than before for another season.

It was growing toward the early autumn twilight when Dick and Mateo dismounted, and they could see dusky figures coming out from the village to jump upon their ponies here and there and begin to collect the grazing herd. It was a point of pride rather than of thrift for the Indians to take good care of their four-legged property. They owned many horses and were rich in the eyes of jealous enemies and in that knowledge they were quite content.

"Every night the herd is driven in and guarded until morning," Mateo said. "But the Sioux have left us long in peace now and our warriors are growing careless. They say that our enemies are fighting elsewhere and have forgotten us, who are such a small village and so far away. When it is my turn to keep guard I do not sleep, but many of the young braves do. I think that the Sioux are only waiting until our hearts and our eyes are closed in the pleasant dream of security—and then they will be upon us again."

As Dick tramped home through the frosty dark, he had a warm, delightful sense of complete well-being. He was splendidly content with the present; he had confidence that he could meet successfully any adventures and hardships that the future might bring. The dark hollow of the valley, the shadowy reach of the great river beyond, the sky above with its shining army of November stars, all seemed to enclose a world of their own, where he and Thomas Garrity and his new friends were to dwell and prosper in happy peace. He did not feel, as once he had done, that he should like to be owner of all those green or wooded acres along the banks of the little winding river. Something, he could not say what, had taught him that there were certain things in that beautiful valley that belonged to every one. Yet he felt that he was the possessor, at that moment, of endless riches, even though all of his worldly goods that could be counted consisted of a ram, a dog, and a silver sixpence.

There had been an arrival during his absence. When Dick opened the door of the cabin he discovered the French trapper, Gil Surette, and his stolid companion sitting by the fire with Thomas Garrity. True to their pledge, they had returned to replace the supplies that had been given them to help their comrade, Melrose, on his way.

"You must have begun to have doubts of our return," Dick heard the Frenchman say, as he came in. "You could not have known the cause of my being so long detained in St. Louis. The truth is I had some little words with the good governor, who does not see all things just as I do. It seems that they have been making new laws that have to do with the trappers and the traders—who ever would have dreamed of such a thing? The life in the woods has a law of its own. The governor even presumes to declare what must be sold to the Indians and what must not; he tried to say what is the proper price for a beaver skin. Bah—men of our calling cannot be hampered by such rules!"

"Did you think that the law would never follow you into the wilderness?" Thomas Garrity asked.

"A few happy years ago, when all this land west of the Mississippi was under the rule of the King of Spain, a brave man might do as he pleased, and need not be bound by any trifling laws. But since Spain gave the lands to France, and France sold them to your thrifty President, things are no longer as they ought to be. The Indians' lives and the Indians' rights must be protected, so your M'sieur President says. Poor man, does he think any one will obey him here beyond the great river? Indians and the law—those are strange comrades! I like not these new American notions!"

"How can the laws make any difference in your trapping?" inquired Dick in wonder.

Ebenezer Wren had paid no attention at all when he had opened the door, and it was only now that Gil Surette turned to greet him with his friendliest, but at the same time his most crafty smile.

"It is true the little furry animals know nothing of whether the King of Spain or the Emperor Napoleon or your good foolish President rules their land; they walk into the traps and give up their warm jackets for poor old Gil Surette with the same kindness," replied the Frenchman. "But the Indians, when you come to buy from them for beads and trinkets, that is another matter. Once let them hear that the President has his eye upon their welfare and they will become more arrogant than ever. They will be demanding guns for skins that once they would have traded for a handful of bits of broken glass. Still"—he shrugged his supple shoulders—"the President is far away; he cannot see into the dense forest or hear very quickly of what goes on in the lodges. The old ways will last for my time, I make no doubt."

They had supper together and, afterward, Surette had insisted that Thomas Garrity should go through the stores that he had brought to make sure that they were a sufficient exchange. Then the whole company sat down again before the fire, and the men pulled out their pipes.

"We will not smoke your tobacco this time, M'sieur Garrity," declared the Frenchman, "since before spring you will have to mix what you have with red willow bark to make it last." He lit a splinter of wood and held it to the evil-smelling bowl. "You should make some tongs of red willow, boy, to lift a hot coal with. It is thus the Indians light their pipes. I hear from M'sieur Garrity that you are learning to be great friends with the Indians. There is wisdom in that, yes, great wisdom." He shook back his long hair and blew out a cloud of smoke.

"In regard to these new laws that I so greatly detest," he remarked after a pause, "there is a matter that concerns you very closely, M'sieur Garrity. But what I have to say of it were better spoken in your private ear."

Privacy in the tiny cabin, occupied at the moment by three very large men and a boy, seemed scarcely possible. But the stout man had laid down his pipe after the first whiff and was now asleep, sitting upright on his three-legged stool with his head against the wall. The energy of his snoring made it certain that he, for the time being, was deaf to all secrets. Dick got up, said that it was time for him to attend to the wants of the sheep, and went out, closing the door behind him. Even before the wooden latch had dropped back into place, he could hear the Frenchman's voice begin in quick, excited talk.

He made sure that the sheep were safe and comfortable and that they were not crowded too closely together in the shelter of the shed behind the great stack. He stopped to rub the woolly head of the ram, who rubbed against him in return. Cormac followed him on his rounds and sniffed carefully at each sheep to be certain, on his own account, that all was well for the night. As the boy and the dog

COMPANION OF THE THUNDER 151

came back toward the house, Dick watched the cheerful red of the fire flickering behind the tiny, square windows and thought how comfortably homelike the little cabin looked, even though it was so unlike anything he had ever dreamed of as home.

He noticed by the moving lights and shadows that some one was striding back and forth before the fireplace and he could hear, even at that distance, voices raised in furious argument. So loud were they that no one heard him as he pulled the latchstring and opened the door.

"You are a madman," the Frenchman was saying, "to go on with this venture when the only hope of success, if hope there is, must lie entirely with the boy."

In the silence that followed Dick stepped across the threshold. The two by the fire did not seem to realize that he might have heard, so intent were they upon the subject of their talk. Ebenezer Wren was still snoring in the corner. Gil Surette turned upon Dick his strange, wolfish smile.

"I have done your comrade the honor of asking him to join me as a partner, and he has done me the compliment of being very angry."

Dick, since the one rude chair and the two stools were occupied, had knelt down by the hearth and was now sitting back on his heels looking up at his guest. At the Frenchman's words, he turned to stare in wonder at Thomas Garrity. He had never seen him angry, but it was certain that he was so now. His face was white; white also were the knuckles of his big hands as they lay clenched on his knees. His deep-set eyes were kindled to a very blaze of wrath, and his voice, when at last he spoke, filled the whole cabin and startled the slumbering Wren into dazed and blinking wakefulness.

"There are some men, among the traders with the Indians, who are honest, but you are not one of them, Gil Surette," he said. "At our first meeting you showed us that with the most open frankness. And you dare to ask us to join you in your ugly business?"

"My business is such that it cannot be carried on in accord with your stiff ideas of honesty," returned Gil Surette coolly. "Who can talk of making an honest bargain with an Indian, who will any day shoot you in the back if the notion is pleasant to him? Some men, as you say, have ideas of honest dealing with our dear, red brothers, and most of them have been murdered for their pains. No, the dangers of my trade are so great that a man must get himself riches in the best and quickest way he can."

The storm of anger had been visibly rising within Thomas Garrity; so that now it was plain he could scarcely keep from getting up from his place to strike the Frenchman down. But in a moment he had mastered himself and was able to speak with at least outward calm.

"For myself, I must refuse your offer. But, as you have said, I have no right to decide for the boy. Let him make his own choice."

CHAPTER XI

THE WHITE PRAIRIE

GIL SURETTE bent his gleaming black eyes upon Dick.

"Will you come with us?" he asked. "Do not believe all that this fellow here says of us. To lead that life of which your comrade seems to think so little, brings a man, in the end, to great fortune."

"Or to sudden death," commented Thomas Garrity.

'To great fortune," repeated the other, unmoved. "A sudden end threatens you far more than it does me, my dear friend, as I have so recently explained to you. You would like riches and adventured, eh, Dick, what boy does not? I will be a rich and honored man with no person asking questions concerning my past, when your M'sieur Garrity, here, is still plodding at the heels of a flock of woolly fools that he calls high-bred sheep. Will you come?"

"No," replied Dick without even stopping to consider the matter. "I will stay here."

He could not leave his good comrade, that was

THE WHITE PRAIRIE 155

a truth so certain that he did not hesitate. There were other things also that weighed with him, the pleasure of his new friendship, the recollection that was still so vividly upon him of that glorious hour of galloping across the prairie. Gil Surette's mode of living could offer him no greater delight than that, he felt sure. He wondered a little over the fact, of which he was beginning to have knowledge, that no matter what way of life you choose, there will be a dozen people to urge you to turn aside from it. He had not thought long over Anthony Robins' persuasions; he did not ponder for a moment now. "No," he said again.

Thomas Garrity's face relaxed and his hands unclenched.

"What could you think of us," he said, "to believe that we would agree to such an offer?"

Gil Surette's eyes narrowed, though he had not lost his smile. "You ask what I think of you, M'sieur Garrity?" he answered. "I think you a man with a long, sour face, who will make no friends nor ever prosper greatly. I think you are a man who, by some sorrow, has let himself be made hard and harsh. You would better have let yourself be made dishonest, as I have become for the same reason. Your unchanging ideas of honest dealing will get you nowhere. And dwelling here in this narrow cabin, you will lead the boy a dull and unhappy life."

He emptied his pipe, stretched his arms, and yawned sleepily.

"Now since each of us knows what the other thinks of him, we need talk no more. Do you refuse us hospitality for the night, honest sir, or may we rest our weary but wicked selves a little before we go onward?"

"I cannot refuse you lodging," agreed Thomas Garrity. "Dick can sleep on the hay that we have stored under the eaves of the sheepshed; so that there will be room for you and your friend in the cabin."

"You will be happy that the boy shall not sleep under the same roof with such men as we," commented the Frenchman, lightly. "Well, well, it may be that you are right. My stout friend, Wren, shall occupy the floor; he could sleep standing if it chanced to be necessary. Dick, my boy, a thousand thanks for your bed. May you sleep as peacefully as I shall!"

Dick was so weary from his long day that he slept dreamlessly under the roof of the shed, but he awoke early, aroused by the restless stamping of the sheep below. As he came near the cabin he saw that, although it was barely light, the two men were already taking their departure. Thomas Garrity stood on the doorstep, making no attempt at a word of farewell. The Frenchman, however, waved his hand gayly as he turned to go down the path.

"You shall hear of us in the spring," he said. "I will stop on my way down the river; I will bring you a beaver skin, Dick; and I will have such stories to tell you, that you will wish many times that you had joined me. For good M'sieur Garrity I have no hopes, but your heart shall thrill to the tale of my adventures."

He was off; the canoe was launched; and, in the dim light of the chill, shivery morning, was quickly out of sight.

They heard of him in the spring; they did, indeed, thrill to the tale of his adventures, but not as he had foretold. In the first warm weather of the early summer, the burly man came paddling down the river alone, gray-faced and wide-eyed with horror of the tragedy he had left behind him. He stopped the excited haste of his journey for only an hour to talk with Dick upon the river bank. He opened one of the packs of furs with which his canoe was laden, and gave the boy a soft, beautiful beaver skin.

"The best one we took," he said to Dick. "Gil Surette put it aside months ago and said it should be for the boy who was not afraid of him. I would not have stopped except that he wished you should have it,"

"And Gil Surette, where is he—and your other comrade?" Dick demanded.

The big man only shook his head. Gil Surette was dead, he managed to tell the boy at last, and so was Melrose, the second trapper. Ebenezer Wren was still too confused, too full, still, of the terror of what he had seen, to describe anything clearly. There had been a sudden flaming forth of savage, Indian rage, a volley of bullets and arrows; then he himself had fled, leaving the other two lying stark upon the snow. The first furs that they had taken had been left at the head of the river; with these he was journeying to St. Louis and then—"No more of the woods for me!" he assured Dick, his voice shaking.

It was plain, so Dick thought, that this man owed his escape to the fact that he was a coward; plain, too, that Gil Surette had died in the face of danger since he scorned to run away. And such was the end of all the Frenchman's great hopes and ambitions, slain by the revengeful fury of the Indians whom he had robbed and bullied; dead in a remote, lost corner of the frozen world. From his manner, his bearing, and the fashion of his speech, it had always been evident that he was a man of good birth and education, holding a place of high honor, perhaps in France or in Canada. Some chance occurrence had embittered and changed him and led him far from home to this unworthy end.

Ebenezer Wren would not stay to rest, not even to eat. He must "go on—go on," he kept repeating. He swung out into the river and, paddling steadily southward, disappeared forever from Dick's view and his knowledge.

All this, however, was months later than that cold November dawn when Gil Surette had set forth so confidently upon his journey. Between that time and the coming of the tragic tidings, Dick and Thomas Garrity were to have strange adventures of their own.

The autumn had lasted so long that Dick began to believe that winter would prove to be very little different, perhaps a little colder, perhaps with somewhat less of the still, golden sunshine, but nothing very harsh or severe. He wondered why Surette and Wren had been in such haste to accomplish their journey northward. Nothing in all of his experience had prepared him for the day upon which the winter really began.

He had gone out with his gun on an afternoon some time later, and had found, as he tramped through the woods, surprisingly little game. It was true that the sky was overcast and the air was singularly chilly, but he could not see how such small changes in the weather could have suddenly driven all the birds and rabbits to cover. He trudged for miles; he sat down and watched behind a log, motionless for a long time; he got up and walked on again, and seemed to find nothing stirring in the silent woods besides himself. Finally he climbed to the rim of the valley, farther from home than he had often journeyed on foot, and came out upon the open prairie. Here at last he found a partridge or two, not crouched in the tufts of long grass, as he had expected, but fluttering toward the forest as though in great haste to seek shelter. Even here, however, the game was difficult to find, so that he had walked a mile or two out into the wide plain before he began to think of turning homeward.

He had not noticed that the sky was growing steadily duller and grayer overhead. He was, therefore, startled when the tall grass about him began suddenly to rustle and a cold wind came roaring across the prairie from the west. With it came a furiously driving cloud of snow, snow so fine and so hard-frozen that it cut his face and blinded him when he tried, for a moment, to stand against it. There was no resisting the wild onslaught of the storm, so he turned and ran before it over the rough ground, catching his feet in the tangled grass whenever he wandered off one of the trampled trails. He could not see more than a few yards ahead, since

THE WHITE PRAIRIE

the dense curtain of snow was now so thick about him that he felt smothered in the swirling whiteness.

If the wind had blown steadily from the west it might have been a guide for him, but it whirled about and buffeted him on every side in turn. In a few minutes he had lost his bearings entirely and was running first in one direction, then in another, without knowing in the least which way led toward home. He tried to stand still for a moment, thinking that the snowstorm was a sudden squall and would pass. But instead of abating, the snow increased and the wind roared more and more fiercely until he could not stand upright, even with his back toward it.

"So this is what the winter is like!" he thought in astonishment, and in a daze he questioned further, "How am I to get home?"

Almost immediately a dark form loomed through the driving white of the storm and Mateo came out into the small circle wherein things were still visible about him.

"To stand still is more dangerous than to be lost," cried the Indian boy above the roar of the wind. "Come quickly."

It cost all of the effort that Dick could muster to keep up with his swiftly moving guide, who knew the way home in spite of the white confusion. After what seemed a long tramp, the way became rougher underfoot, and the friendly shelter of the forest gathered them in from the furious threat of the blizzard. They walked slower and more easily, and finally came down the hill into the valley. There the snow was falling more peacefully, but the slopes and the meadows already were white.

"How did you happen to be on the prairie, too?" Dick asked. It was the first moment that he was master of enough breath to ask a question.

"I saw you go over the hill and knew that you did not guess the storm was coming," answered Mateo. "If I had not been so near when the snow began, I should never have come upon you. We should both have wandered about all night or, if the storm held, until we both perished."

"If you could not find me, you could at least have found the way back," said Dick. "You seem to know your way across the prairie blindfold."

"I did not intend to come back without you," returned the Indian, simply, and added before Dick could answer, "If you do not climb the trail quickly to your lodge on the hill, you will find the way very deep in snow."

The winter was certainly something far different from what Dick had expected. Fortunately, the cabin had been well chinked with clay and banked with earth, and the chimney of the fireplace had been finished with great labor; so that there was no dan-

THE WHITE PRAIRIE 163

ger that the householders would freeze, no matter how cold the weather. The sheep were well provided for, although there were days when even they seemed to shiver in their woolly coats and to look abroad with troubled eyes upon a harsh, frozen world very unlike their mild-weathered Ireland. The big ram alone seemed to enjoy the cold, and he and Dick and Cormac frisked and tumbled on the snow until their blood tingled and the boy's cheeks glowed.

"If the Indians do not freeze in their lodges, we should not in our stout cabin," Thomas Garrity declared.

The little windows were closed with wooden shutters, since there was no glass for them, and the wind roared down the chimney with a force that often scattered the firebrands across the floor. Yet on blustery evenings the thick-walled cabin was a cozy place, with the blazing fire, the deerskin rugs on the floor, the gay blankets covering the two bunks, and, on the rude semblance of a chimney-piece, Mr. Noah standing forth in all the glory of his green coat, his red waistcoat, and his smiling face. Hiram Evarts' little daughter would have been happy to know how brave a show her gift was making as the sole ornament of the cabin.

Thomas Garrity sat in the single chair through the long evenings, smoking his pipe and bringing stories of every sort from the rich storehouse of his memory. He had more than one eager listener. Katequa and her brother at first had refused to enter the cabin, being in open dread of the tall, serious man who was Dick's companion; but little by little Dick's accounts of his friend had overcome their aloofness. It came to be their habit at last to sit by the fire almost every evening and listen, with Dick's help as interpreter, to Thomas Garrity's talk.

It was the Indian boy who, at this time, helped Dick over a great difficulty. He had of long wondered what he should call his older comrade, since his first habit of addressing him as "Mr. Garrity," seemed out of place as the two grew to be such close friends. But there was a certain stateliness about the Irishman that made a shortening of his name seem difficult. Mateo, although he had mastered the short syllables of "Dick Martin," had such trouble with saying "Thomas Garrity," that he was forced at last to shorten the name to "Tom." And Tom their good friend became, to all three of them.

One night Katequa had looked up at the figure of Mr. Noah and asked what sort of a totem was that which they guarded so carefully above their firestone.

"That figure is only a child's toy," said Thomas Garrity, "but it stands for a great story."

With Dick's help he proceeded to relate to the

THE WHITE PRAIRIE 165

Indian boy and girl the history of the Flood and of Noah's share therein.

Mateo nodded quickly when he had finished.

"We know that tale also," he declared, "although with us the telling is not quite the same. The men of earth had all grown wicked and did not heed the commands of the Great Spirit, so that first he sent darkness over the land and the people were filled with great terror. Finally they saw a long gleam of light on the horizon. 'It is the day come at last,' they cried, 'the Great Spirit has not seen our sins after all, we can go on as we did before!' But it was not the sun, it was the white crest of a great wave, a mountain of water, that came rolling in and broke over them with a deafening roar."

In his eagerness to tell the story he had spoken too quickly for Dick to follow and now must go back and, with Katequa's help, make clear what he had been saying. When Dick and Thomas Garrity had understood all that he had told, he went on:

"The waters grew deeper and deeper, the people fled before them; they gathered at last upon a high, red rock, their final refuge. But the waters came up and up and drowned them all; for they were very wicked. Only one person was saved, a girl who had in all her life done no such wrong as the others. As she stood on the summit of the rock, a great eagle flew overhead, she caught his huge claws, and he carried her away. After the flood went down she married the eagle, and their children were the beginning of a new race, a people who, like the eagle, must abide in wild forest places, who live by hunting, and who perish in captivity. It was so my sister got her name; many Indian girls are named after the mother of the race, Katequa. the eagle's maiden."

Mateo stopped, evidently surprised that he had spoken so long. He looked inquiringly from Dick to Thomas Garrity to see whether they had understood his tale.

"I have followed most of it," Dick assured him. "Go on. Is there more?"

"There is this one thing more. That rock where all the wicked perished lies far to the north of us, near the head of the great river. It is the one spot in the whole country where the Indians do not make war, tribe against tribe. Out of that red stone is made the pipes that men smoke together as a sign of peace, and from beyond the prairies and the mountains, from the shores of the Big Water even, the warriors come to get the pipestone. The Great Spirit has commanded that upon that one spot there should be peace for all time. When that peace is broken, the Indian race will perish."

After that the talk was often of greater and graver things about the cabin fire. The Indian boy and girl were never tired of hearing more about that Great Spirit whom all their race worshiped with such devout hearts but with so little knowledge.

"We must go very carefully," Thomas Garrity told Dick, who was eager to relate to them the legends of saints and miracles that he had heard from Bridget Anne. "Do not confuse them by telling them of things that they cannot yet understand."

So it was through the simple, stirring stories of the Old Testament that Thomas Garrity led them slowly toward the great truths of the New.

"I like that tale of the man who set up his lodges after they had been destroyed, while his enemies looked on and laughed," was Mateo's comment on the history of Nehemiah. "He was a truly brave warrior!"

This was his favorite, but Katequa preferred hearing of the great wisdom and the high courage of Daniel.

"I love to hear of that man who went down into the wild beasts' den," she said, "and who cried, 'Oh, King, live forever,' from among the lions, because he knew that the king loved him and he was not afraid."

It had not been difficult to make her understand what lions were, since their fierce kindred lurked in the broken country along some of the rivers; but it needed long explanation to make clear the nature of a king. An Indian chief has no pride of place; he lives the same life and performs the same labor as the other men of his tribe and is only distinguished by the responsibility of being the leader in times of difficulty. Both the boy and girl, however, were quick to understand, to grasp even greater and more unthought-of things than the nature of a king. Dick and Thomas Garrity made slow and cautious progress with their teaching, although the real missionary, he who had begun the work, was the smiling little Mr. Noah in his green coat and yellow trousers.

There were various small tasks to be accomplished on these winter evenings, to the pleasant accompaniment of talk and laughter. Dick was much entertained by Katequa's astonishment the first time she saw him get out his leather housewife, thread a needle with linen twist, and fall to sewing a button on a tattered shirt. She exclaimed with wonder and delight as the bright steel thing went in and out in the twinkling firelight. She was used only to sinew thread and bone needles. Clumsy as they are, they have such value in the Indians' eyes that, when a great chief dies, they are among the precious household effects that must be buried with him. So when, at the end of his work, Dick presented the needle and the spool of thread to her, Katequa was overcome with awe and joy.

"I have more," he assured her when she hesitated. He showed her the row of spools and the bit of cloth stuck full of needles. Elizabeth Evarts had guessed both shrewdly and kindly when she realized how valuable such articles would be in a frontier household. Even Mateo was interested and excited over the wonderful gift, and, when they departed homeward with their new possession wrapped in a piece of buckskin, he was as anxious as his sister lest the treasure be lost.

The cold grew steadier. The Des Moines river disappeared under a covering of ice and snow, although there were places where the swift water ran close to the surface, since the tumbling current was reluctant to freeze. The wide blue expanse of the Mississippi began to run full with cakes and sheets of floating ice, which moved more and more slowly as the river gradually closed, and at last turned into a vast field of unbroken white.

One evening as Dick came out of the cabin at the darkening edge of twilight, he saw Cormac in a running, snapping fight with what the boy took to be a lean, gray dog. At his shout the dark beast slunk away, with Cormac snarling at his heels.

Mateo came across the snow to stand beside Dick as he stood peering into the dark.

"Call back your dog," he said. "If he follows that wolf into the wood he will be torn to pieces by the rest of the pack. The creatures are cowards when they are alone, but when they are together, or later in the winter, when they are colder and hungrier, they will attack anything. It is a sign that we are to have a harsh winter when these gray beasts come skulking down the hill so early."

Cormac came back at Dick's whistle, little the worse for his encounter, but bristling and growling to himself at the recollection of this new danger to his precious sheep.

Mateo would not stay long beside the fire in the cabin, for he said he was sleepy, having watched the horses in his proper turn all the night before.

"As the winter goes on, we fear our enemies less and less," he told them. "Once the deep drifts lie in the valley, they cannot drive away our horses, and we feel safe. We think of them huddling together in the cold and blowing their fingers about their lodge fires as we are doing. But just now the snow is still thin and hard and they may steal upon us any night. I do not believe that they have forgotten us."

When he got up to go, Dick went out with him to have another look at the sheep. "I may be gone an hour or more, Tom," he said. "I meant to put down a fresh bed of straw, and there has been no time for it until to-night."

It was a cold night, with a brilliant moon, but with clouds driving across the sky, so that now and then

THE WHITE PRAIRIE 171

the flood of light was completely blotted out. As they stood at the top of the trail, their shadows lay clear and black upon the snow.

"I had only my shadow for company when I kept guard last night," said Mateo. "The others who watched with me were very alert for an hour and then crept back to their lodge fires, telling each other that the Sioux will never come in such cold. The men of our race have long memories for the avenging of wrongs and short ones for the chances of danger."

"If the others do not watch, why should you?" Dick asked.

Mateo hesitated a moment, staring away across the Mississippi, now a level plain of snow-covered ice. He was about to tell the closest secret of his heart to his dearest friend.

"My father was a great chief," he said slowly. "He guarded the safety of the tribe as his highest possession. Even though I am not old enough to stand in his place, I think often that I must do what I can to keep the village safe, with the little courage and the small wisdom that he taught me. But oh, I am tired and sleepy to-night."

He was off quickly across the hill before another word could be said. Dick walked down the slope in the opposite direction to look at the marks of Cormac's scuffle in the snow. He had left the dog behind by the fire, but he could follow alone the footprints of the wolf where it had loped away, circling first toward the crest of the bluff, before it had taken cover in the woods above. As he stood listening, he heard a long, quavering howl lifted from the black forest. In quick silence he slipped behind a clump of bushes to watch whether the gray thief would come back to snuff about the sheepfold again. He sat very still for a long time, while the moon went under a cloud and came out once more. His hands and feet were stiff with cold, so that he was about to move, when something rustled, very gently, a few yards away, in the underbrush on the face of the bluff.

In the darkness of the hidden moon, something had been stealing up the hill. Was it the wolf again? Dick held his breath as he watched and listened. It was no wolf. A figure rose upright among the bushes and moved up the slope, making no sound except for the soft squeak of the snow under moccasined feet. A tall warrior crossed a patch of moonlight as the clouds drifted away and stood revealed so clearly that Dick could see the bright feathers of his headdress, the curve of his bow, and the tight folds of his buffalo blanket. They were all of a color and cut different from the garments of his friends of the Sac-and-Fox tribe. He could even see the streaks of gaudy paint on the man's

THE WHITE PRAIRIE

forehead and cheeks and along his bared bow-arm. War paint it was, as Dick well knew. This was a Sioux warrior, the dreaded enemy come at last!

The boy never knew what sound he made that caught the Indian's ear, whether he had let out his pent-up breath too suddenly, or whether by some other tiny movement he had betrayed his presence behind the bush. Like a flash the Sioux vanished into the shade of an overhanging hickory tree, where he was hidden as completely as though he had never existed. Yet Dick could fairly feel those black eyes peering out from the shadow. The boy and the warrior each crouched in his own place, each intently aware of the other, and each waiting for his adversary to make the first move.

CHAPTER XII

THE SHADOWY SIOUX

AS Dick crouched, waiting, behind the clump of bushes, his mind seemed to be as clear and cool as the sparkling cold of the moonlight night. He felt sure that, had he not chanced to fall into the Indian's way, the Sioux warrior would have had no hostile intentions, perhaps not even a thought toward the dwellers in the little cabin. Indians knew so little of sheep that they would attach no value to them; and such Indians as the Sioux, dwelling far to the north or the west of the Des Moines valley, could have small interest in murdering the two lone white people who had settled there. No, the Sac-and-Fox village and the band of horses were plainly the objects of this raid, whose foremost scout had come so silently up the hill.

Now, as he looked down, there came a second shadow stealing after the first, across an open slope below him. Perhaps some signal, unseen by Dick, passed between the first warrior and the second, for the moving figure was suddenly blotted out in some dark hiding place of rock or tree trunk. Then a twig snapped lower down, in the bushes at the water's edge, as though a third Indian had stolen forth and been stopped by a sign from above.

It was probable, so he thought quickly, that these men, with others behind them, were intending to cross the high land between the Mississippi and the Des Moines, to drop down to the bed of the smaller stream, and to make their way toward the village under cover of the banks and the snow-wreathed willow trees. Possibly there were other warriors hidden on the forest-covered bluff above the village, so that suddenly two files of whooping braves were to rush together upon the sleeping lodges in the meadow.

At that thought, Dick all of a sudden began to be afraid. It was not fear for himself that swept him with such a gust of panic; it was the alarming sense of responsibility, the knowledge that upon what he did now hung the result of the intended attack. He must warn his friends in the Sac-and-Fox village, but how was he to do it? What if he should make the wrong decision? Such waiting and pondering breed terror. The warm, red light shone through the chinks of the cabin windows, giving notice of the peace and comfort in which Thomas Garrity was sitting by the fire within. If it were only possible to ask his advice!

It was this very picture of Thomas Garrity that

calmed his terror and once more cleared his brain. Presently, so the boy knew, his comrade might begin to wonder where Dick had gone, he would open the door, see the footprints in the snow, and follow them, walking unarmed across the moonlit open, straight toward the Indian's hiding place. And the Sioux, rather than be discovered, would shoot him dead. That was certain. It was this knowledge and the fact that a cloud had once more blotted out the moon that spurred him to decisive action.

He might have known that, with the first moment of darkness, the Indian would act also. But his racing wits had failed to note this possibility, so that the two who had waited so long, each for the other, now darted forth together and came into violent collision on the summit of the ridge. The snow was so hard and smooth that neither had a steady balance, and they clung to each other in strange and unwilling embrace. Slipping and staggering, but still holding together, they stumbled over the edge of the ridge and went rolling down the frozen hillside toward the bank of the Des Moines. The slope, just here, was smooth and open, scarcely obstructed by trees or bushes. Dick could feel the bare flesh of the Indian's arm pressed against his face; he could feel the man's chest heaving against his shoulder and the strain of the other's great thigh muscles as he struggled to find footing. Since there was nothing to

THE SHADOWY SIOUX

stop them, the two went in one plunging fall from the top of the ridge to the bottom, and ended in a thicket of thorn bushes at the foot of the hill. The Indian's weapons, knife, bow, shield, and lance, had all gone clattering and sliding away into the dark during that headlong tumble down the frozen slope.

The warrior's greater weight carried him farther into the bushes than Dick, who jerked himself free in an instant. There was an astonished grunt from the Sioux as the long thorns pierced his buckskin shirt and tore his skin; this was the only sound he uttered. Dick, though still bewildered by the fall, got to his feet, plunged through the willows, and dropped over the river bank before the other had time even to sit up and try to peer through the darkness. It was, mercifully, a very big cloud that had drifted over the moon.

With Dick lay the great advantage of knowing the ground. He could tell, even in the dark, just where the bushes were thinnest, where the bank was high enough to shelter him as he ran along the edge of the ice below, where he could cut off a curve in the stream by slipping over a willow-covered headland. He was well on his way with his message of warning to the Sac-and-Fox village before he even heard the Sioux warrior go crashing through the underbrush to reach the river.

A mile is a strangely long way to run in the dark, with a deadly enemy behind and a fitful moon overhead to puzzle or betray with its uncertain light. Dick could hear vague sounds behind him of more than one person struggling through the tangled willow thickets, and once he caught the crash of breaking ice and the splash of water. Where the current ran near the shore, the covering of ice was still thin and brittle, so that some unsuspecting brave had gone blundering through into the deadly cold water that ran below. Even in the shock of the icy bath, the Indian had made no outcry. Dick, forced to stop for a moment to lean against a tree and ease his bursting lungs, had a sudden strange wonder whether this silent company could any of it be real.

He had reached the wide sweep of the Des Moines, where it curved in a great semicircle, with the Sac-and-Fox village at the center. He might follow the shore farther and come within a hundred yards of the silent lodges, but it was a long distance thither, while a far shorter way was straight across the unsheltered open. Were his pursuers far enough behind for him to risk the run across the white expanse of the meadow; or would some marksman from the underbrush let fly an arrow that would put an end to his errand for all time? It was worth risking, he decided. The moon came out of the clouds in serene splendor as he ran forward over the snow.

A spent arrow flitted past him and dropped with a tiny clatter on the frozen crust. Otherwise there was no sound save the crunching of his running feet, feet so slow and heavy now, in spite of the mad need for haste. Another arrow swept past him. This was not a spent shot, for the shaft stood upright and quivering in the hard snow.

How peacefully the village slept in the white meadow under the white moon. He could see the dark, pointed lodges and the smoldering red of a little watchfire at the edge of the circle of silent dwellings. Whoever had been keeping guard beside that fire was evidently now asleep. Between Dick and the village the herd of horses had spread across the meadow, a few of them still close to the fire where they had been driven at nightfall, the rest scattered here and there over the open spaces and toward the river. Not many yards from him a dilapidated old mare was standing asleep on three legs, her heavy old head nodding slowly and, in the bright moonlight, her dense black shadow nodding with it.

A sudden red-hot finger seemed to touch his temple, as another arrow shot whistling past. He raised his hand and felt a trickle of blood over his fingers. He gave up the effort to stumble farther and lifted his voice in a husky shout.

"Mateo," he cried. "Mateo!"

His call had sounded so cracked and uncertain that it seemed as though no one would ever hear it. He put both hands to his mouth and, with one last effort of his spent lungs, he sent forth the pulsating war cry that Mateo had taught him.

The sleeping world before him woke to startled life. A horse wheeled and snorted; a voice from the lodges answered his call; and black figures came pouring out into the light of the little fire. Then, in a moment, there rose above everything a terrible sound, dropping from the hills above, echoing along the river bank behind him, the hideous warwhoop of the Sioux.

"That is all I can do," he thought dimly. "I wonder if that was Mateo who answered. I wonder what will happen to Katequa."

He was dizzy with fatigue and with the aching wound in his head, so that he swayed where he stood watching in the snow. Vaguely he saw mounted figures come hurtling down from the wooded hill, and was aware of a file of leaping shadows that came out of the willow trees at his right. He was moving slowly back to take shelter among the trees once more when one Indian stopped and faced him. He swung his heavy, pointed war club, measuring

THE SHADOWY SIOUX

the distance for a throw. At that moment a shot rang out from the village, the first shot fired. The warrior dropped, his painted war club still swinging from his hand. The shot had been a chance one, nor was Dick more than dimly conscious of what he had escaped.

He came into the dark shade of the wooded river bank and sat down upon a log. As he was unarmed there was little hope of his taking any successful part in the battle that was now raging up and down among the lodges. Now that his warning was given he was almost too spent even to think of what would happen next. He put his whirling head down on his knees and sat listening to the strange tumult, still wondering whether he might not be dreaming it.

After a little he found his swimming head was growing steadier and that the handful of snow he had laid upon the bleeding wound had, in a measure, stopped the pain. A new sound caught his attention, the steady pounding of countless unshod hoofs coming across the meadow. He got to his uncertain feet and came out into an open trail through the willows, a broad path where the horses went daily to drink at the river. Across the open the whole band was galloping down upon him, driven by a handful of yelling Sioux braves. They were waving their buffalo robes, and swinging firebrands about their heads in blazing circles and with a wide scattering of sparks. Since it had been impossible to surprise the village and make off with the horses, the enemy were seeking to drive the herd down into the river, where, on the thin ice above the current, they would break through and be whirled to destruction.

Dick's weariness and pain seemed to fall from him in an instant. At the center of the line of plunging horses he could see the black leader, with wide nostrils and flying mane, thundering down upon him.

"If Cormac were only here," he thought desperately.

And then, almost as he thought it, there was Cormac, racing up from the river like a streak of yellow lightning, and flinging himself upon the flying black horse. As a much smaller boy and an awkward puppy had once turned the struggling flock of sheep when they sought to plunge to their death, so did the two, grown older and wiser, face and try to turn the tenfold more furious charge of the maddened horses that broke upon them now.

Dick had torn off his coat and was waving it over his head and yelling as frantically as the warriors behind. At Cormac's leap the leading horse had flinched and swerved, but had then come on again, while Cormac rolled over and over among the stamping hoofs. The dog was at Dick's side again instantly, escaped as by a miracle from those trampling feet; he was snarling and leaping, and finally yelping in loud and joyous defiance. The big leader was upon them. The yellow fury of a dog sprang at him again; Dick waved his coat wildly and shouted with what was left of his hoarse voice. Whether the horse knew that voice even above the mad uproar of yells and yelps and pounding hoofs, whether it was Cormac's final leap that turned him, no one would ever know. He swung aside from the open trail and plunged into the willows at the right. The whole herd followed, slackening their speed in the tangled thickets and scattering among the trees. Only one clumsy colt blundered into Dick in the dark, knocking him off his feet and rolling him into the bushes.

"Down, Cormac, be still," he ordered in a stern whisper, holding the dog close to him.

The wild riders had flung themselves down the trail, had checked, and were now galloping back and forth, shouting and waving their torches, in a last effort to drive the herd into the river. But the clinging, supple willow branches made speed impossible and destroyed any hope of getting the scattered band together again. The shouts were suddenly hushed, the torches were blotted out and the Sioux disappeared as silently as those shadows from which they had issued in the beginning.

The attack of a party of Indians is like the attack of an eagle, a furious swoop, a desperate snatching and tearing with cruel claws, and a swift skimming away, either with the intended prey or without it. The Sioux had failed in their hope of surprising a sleeping village; they had lost the herd of horses in the riverside thickets. Now, after stopping only to gather up their fallen comrades, they were fleeing to the hills, with not a thought of returning to the attack. Lights moved back and forth among the lodges; fires blazed up; and the shrill excited voices of the women took the place of the shouting of the fighting men. The battle was over.

Dick got up giddily and made his way down to the edge of the stream. Some stumbling pony had broken through into the shallow water near the bank, leaving a jagged-edged pool, as black as ink against the snowy surface of the river. Here Dick bathed his bleeding head, while Cormac drank in large, contented laps, although the water was so cold that needles of ice were already forming in it.

Then the two moved off toward home, Dick with so slow and stumbling a gait that Cormac kept looking back inquiringly, his eyes full of wonder why his usually eager master did not hurry. It seemed that the same thought was in both their minds: Had any harm come to Thomas Garrity?

In that long file of silent warriors which had

come over the hill and passed so close to the cabin, was every man too intent upon the coming battle to pause on the crest of the hill? Or had one stopped, peered in at the window, silently lifted the latch——? Dick was vaguely anxious to know whether harm had come to Mateo, whether Katequa was safe; but there was room for only one definite thought in his reeling brain and that thought was of his comrade in the cabin on the hill.

It had seemed a long way when he had come up the river; it seemed twice as long as he made his weary, unsteady way back again. More than once he looked up at the moon still appearing and disappearing among the sailing clouds. He had thought it must be almost setting by now, but no, it still rode high overhead. So little time had passed, although so much had happened.

He passed the last curve of the river bank and struggled up the trail, which had never seemed so steep as now. There was the cabin above him, safe and undisturbed, with the welcome red light showing behind the windows and the comfortable white smoke going up steadily in the moonlight. He and Cormac were on the doorstep; Dick's fumbling hand was on the latch. He was so weak and weary he could hardly lift it and push open the door.

Thomas Garrity sat just where he had left him, in the light of the fire, with a book in his hand. He looked up over his big, horn spectacles as Dick stood on the threshold.

"The sheep must have wanted a deal of looking to," he said. "You have been gone a long time."

Dick stood for a moment in the darkness of the doorway. He must be very careful, he thought mistily, not to startle Thomas Garrity too much. He realized that he must be an alarming sight with his clothes torn and caked with snow, and with blood trickling down his face. It was Cormac, rushing in and trying to tell Thomas Garrity that something was wrong, who gave the older man the first inkling of what had occurred.

"What is it?" he cried, getting out of his chair, as Dick came across to sit down unsteadily upon the stool.

"It is nothing bad," the boy assured him, trying to gather his staggering wits. "Over at the village——"

"I heard some shouting," said Thomas Garrity, as Dick paused. "I thought the Indians were having one of their dances; you cannot tell much from sounds a mile away. I opened the door and Cormac ran out, but I thought all the while that you were with the sheep. What is it, lad?" he cried, as Dick swayed upon the stool. "What has happened?"

Dick laughed. It was at a strange fancy that had just come into his whirling head. The Frenchman had said to Thomas Garrity: "I think you are a man with a long, sour face, who will make no friends." And now Thomas Garrity's face might be Bridget Anne's, so full was it of kindness, affection, and terrified concern. He felt that no one could have such a friend as he had in Thomas Garrity. But the laugh sent a wave of giddiness over him, so that the room, the warm firelight, Mr. Noah in his green coat, and that kind, troubled face all swam together before him.

"It is—it is so good to get home!" was all he managed to say, and slid off the stool into unconsciousness.

CHAPTER XIII

A BARGAIN IN GOOD LUCK

IT seemed very strange to Dick to be lying idly in his bunk, watching Thomas Garrity build the fire on the rough hearth. Making the fire had always been his own task, so that he could not help thinking that Thomas Garrity was not doing it so well as he. But the yellow flames kindled at last; the rude chimney began to roar; the hearthstone was brushed clean with a wild turkey's wing, and Thomas Garrity straightened his long back and turned about to Dick.

He smiled with relief as he saw the boy's eyes, clear and steady, looking back at him from the pillow. Dick had passed through two days and nights of feverish pain and restlessness, and of babbling talk of which he was vaguely conscious, but which he could not control. No sick person ever had a more careful and tender nurse than Thomas Garrity. It did not seem possible that such big, heavy hands could be so deft at changing bandages or at moving a bruised and aching body that could not lie still long on the hard bed. Once Dick had come out of some queer maze of feverish dreaming and had heard Thomas Garrity singing. He was sitting beside the bunk and humming, very low, but in that rich, thrilling voice that the boy had not heard since the night on shipboard, when they had sat together in the warm starlight and had first learned to be friends.

"Bendemeer's Stream," he muttered and, as Thomas Garrity slipped into the rhythm of the well-loved melody, the boy took firm hold of his friend's rough coat sleeve to keep himself from drifting back into the tormented nightmare out of which he had come. Finally he slid into comfortable sleep.

Now, on this cold, sunny morning of the third day, he found his head clear, and, moving easily at last under the blankets, he realized that strength was coming back. Cormac, who throughout his master's illness had lain on the floor beside the bunk, following every troubled move with dark, distressed eyes, now jumped up joyfully and came pressing his tawny head against the pillow and thrusting his cold nose against Dick's neck. "He is better," he seemed to be signaling with his joyously waving brush of a tail. "Now we can all feel safe again!"

Thomas Garrity looked as delighted as Cormac, but he said rather less. He went forward with his preparations for breakfast and finally brought a steaming wooden bowl to Dick's bedside. It might have been hard to lie so long on a mattress of cedar boughs, but it was glorious to appease the first ravenous appetite of convalescence on savory partridge broth.

Thomas Garrity waited until the bowl was nearly empty and then spoke in his old, severe tone.

"Don't you know," he said slowly, "that there is nothing more wrong a white man can do, than to take part in the warfare of one Indian tribe against another?"

Dick grinned happily as he sat up against the pillow and went on gulping down his soup. There could be no more certain sign that he was better than that Thomas Garrity should begin to be stern with him again. He had quite emptied the bowl before he answered.

"No one can desert his friends," he declared. "And," he added in surprised questioning, "how did you know what happened that night?"

"A boy does not come home with an arrow wound plowed through the side of his head, and with his whole body plastered with purple and yellow bruises, without there being some reason for it," returned Thomas Garrity. "You talked a good deal, also, when you were the most ill, though I did not under-

A BARGAIN IN GOOD LUCK 191

stand all that you said about broken ice and horses. Now suppose you tell me just what headlong folly you ran into. Cormac has done his best to give me a full account of the affair, but I am a stupid old man and did not follow just what he was trying to say."

Dick carefully licked the last, rich flavor from the spoon, gave up the bowl, and lay down again. As he related to his comrade the full tale of what had happened on that strange night, he wondered if he had not dreamed it, although the heaviness of his bandaged head gave ample proof that it had all been true. Thomas Garrity, as he listened, was not able to keep up the show of his stern manner.

"And to think that I sat here in peace and safety by the fire while all this went on outside," he interrupted hotly at one point. "Cormac was uneasy and troubled, and when I opened the door to try to see what delayed you, he was off like a bullet from a gun. But the whole affair passed so silently, and I was so sure that you were with the sheep, that I came back to the fire again. One often hears guns fired, or shouting from the village, when they are having their ceremonial dances. But go on, lad, go on."

He shook his head fiercely, again, as Dick came to the end of his story.

"If I had only been with you," he repeated, and then checked himself suddenly. "But as I said," he ended, "no white man should take part in these wars of the savages."

"But the Indians are our friends," Dick still maintained stoutly, and knew, from the glint in the older man's deep eyes, that they were really of one heart in the matter.

"Well, well, it is best to say as little of the affair as possible," Thomas Garrity declared at last. "But I wish we knew whether that boy and girl were safe!"

He carried away the bowl, but Dick noticed that he put it down on the table absently and stood looking into the fire for a long time.

"Dick," he said at last with sudden directness, "where did you learn to be so loyal to friends?"

"Why—why," the boy stammered in some surprise, "from you—from Cormac—from——" A strange truth suddenly leaped into his mind, and looking up, he saw that the same knowledge had come to Thomas Garrity also. "I think I have learned the most of friendship from the Indians themselves!"

He turned the new idea over and over in his mind. "Michael More and Bridget Anne were good friends to me, but they had to go on and leave me behind. The sailor, he was a good friend, too, but

A BARGAIN IN GOOD LUCK 193

he could not keep me with him because he said he was no sort of man for a boy to live with. And Peggy Reilly, who was a friend to my mother once——" He winced even now at the memory of the wound that sharp tongue had made, the day when he found that no one wanted him. "No, I will not think of her. And there was the little spinning woman, she was good to me. But—yes, it is true, besides you and Cormac I have never had friends that I have loved so dearly or that I have been so sure of as Mateo and Katequa."

He thought of how Katequa had come to warn him of the danger from the French trapper; how Mateo had gone out in the snowstorm on the prairie to bring him home; how they had taught him to paddle, to fish, to do a dozen things that made his life safer and easier. He could be quite certain that he had no better friends in the world than they. No wonder every instinct within him had bidden him go to warn them when danger threatened. He would do the same a hundred times, in spite of Thomas Garrity's severity and his warnings about white men and Indian warfare. He smiled within himself at the knowledge that Thomas Garrity's sternness was pure humbug.

It was not until the first day that he was able to go out to tend the sheep, that he had any news as to the welfare of his Indian friends. As he walked slowly and stiffly along the path from the cabin door to the sheep pen, he saw Katequa coming up the trail from the river. Her face looked unusually sober, but broke into smiles when she saw him.

"You have not heard, perhaps," she told him excitedly, "that we had an attack from the Sioux. They actually rode in among our lodges, but some one had shouted a warning in time, so that our warriors were awake."

"Was Mateo hurt?" Dick asked quickly.

A little—a Sioux knife had gashed his thigh, she told him. But he was mending now and soon would be able to walk again. The warriors were all much relieved that the attack had been beaten off with so little loss. Even the horses were all safe, she assured him further. They had somehow scattered among the willows, so that it had been impossible for the enemy to drive them away.

Dick stood faltering and embarrassed, unable to feign any great astonishment at what she told him and equally unable to tell her what he, on his part, knew of that night's struggle. Even had he wished to, he could never have found words to describe his share in that adventure. She seemed to feel hurt at his want of interest, for her smile faded, and she said briefly:

"Mateo has asked often to see you. I could not leave him sooner than this to tell you so."

A BARGAIN IN GOOD LUCK 195

"I will come to-morrow," he returned, with such hearty good will that her cheerfulness was somewhat restored.

"That was not all that I came to tell you," she went on, and at the thought of her other errand, all of her irrepressible smiles broke out again. "You are to have a visitor, Waponjea, the wife of the chief. She has been so curious to see your house, now that you have finished building it, that she cannot wait longer. She will ask to taste your white sugar; we ourselves have never seen anything but maple sugar. She will wish to look at everything in your cabin, and then turn it upside down and look at the under side. She has sat for hours and watched me sew with the needle you gave me, and she has asked me a hundred times if you had another and if you would part with such a beautiful thing."

Having given him warning of the intended visit, she flashed him a last smile and went away down the snowy path.

In the course of an hour, as Katequa had promised, there came up the trail, first Waponjea herself, muffled in many fur wrappings, then a motley collection of very old and very young attendants, and last an ancient warrior leading one pony and followed by two more. Indians do not have servants, but their lodges are often filled with dependent relatives, old women, or ancient, worn-out warriors, who have no squaws and no lodges of their own, who live on the bounty of the head of the household, and who do the hard work of the daily life. As Dick looked over the group gathered about the doorstep, he could imagine that, of the thin old women, one might be Waponjea's mother, one her grandmother, and one her mother-in-law, but, since age is difficult to guess in any Indian beyond the prime of life, he could not in the least tell which was which. The limping old man with the horses was possibly her father or her grandfather. Not one of them said a word as he opened the door, but stared at him with steady, black eyes, and then, as many of them as could accomplish it, but still without speaking, came crowding into the cabin.

The great dame was all smiles and graciousness, however, when she had been greeted by Thomas Garrity and had been shown all the various articles that the cabin contained. She examined and fingered everything, giving once in a while a grunt of whole-souled admiration at the brightness of a copper pan or the color of a gay wool blanket. She was dressed in a really beautiful robe of white wolfskins, with such a wealth of beads, necklaces, and swinging metal trinkets that she made a sound like sleigh bells when she moved. Her brown face was wreathed in smiles and was further decorated with

A BARGAIN IN GOOD LUCK

streaks of vermilion paint, to grace the ceremony of the occasion. She conspicuously lacked the simple dignity of Katequa and the other women of Mateo's lodge, but, despite her vanity and her evident love of gaudy possessions, she seemed a direct and kindly soul. Dick thought better of her when suddenly a choked wail came from beneath her muffling buffalo robe, and it was revealed that under her outer wrappings she carried on her back a tiny, beady-eyed pappoose. She hushed and fondled the little thing upon her knee until its whimperings ceased and, with the tears still standing upon its fat cheeks, it began staring about the cabin with an eager curiosity so like its mother's that Dick could not forbear laughing.

Waponjea laughed in return. She seemed to be delighted with all that she had seen and to enjoy greatly Thomas Garrity's manner of grave politeness and his calling her "madame," even though she could understand no word of what he said. To Dick, who knew enough of her language for halting conversation, she now explained the object of her visit.

Was it possible that he really possessed such another treasure as the one he had given Katequa, that beautiful, steel instrument that went without effort in and out of a piece of buckskin? Dick brought out Elizabeth's Evarts' housewife and showed her that he had not one, but several needles more, while she exclaimed with wonder that any one person should be master of such great wealth.

If he would part with one needle, she explained, she would present him with an adequate gift in return. Her husband, the chief of the tribe, was a rich man and would give her anything she wanted. Would he exchange the needle for a horse?

Very gravely, yet in dreadful fear lest he should laugh aloud at the extraordinary inequality of the bargain, Dick translated her offer to Thomas Garrity. He looked through the open door and noticed, again, that the old man who had come with Waponjea had brought, not one, but three horses. And he had wished for a horse with all the ardent desire that a boy can feel. Was it possible that she would offer them all?

"You must make what bargain you think best," Thomas Garrity said when Dick explained her request. Seeing them in consultation, Waponjea became panic-stricken lest they decide to reject her offer.

"I will give you two," she offered and, since Dick seemed still to be hesitating, "Three," she cried in desperation.

"I could never sell you a needle for three horses," exclaimed Dick. Mistaking his meaning, she answered sadly. "I am afraid my husband would not

A BARGAIN IN GOOD LUCK 199

let me have more than three horses, but there is a very old mare I might beg of him, we could say it was three horses and a half I can give you."

It was no wonder, he thought, that such men as Gil Surette and his comrades found it tempting beyond resistance to defraud the Indians, when they were as innocently eager as this for anything they wanted, and so unskilled at bargaining.

Waponjea's face fell, for she did not understand his hesitation and observed, "I am afraid three horses and a half are all that I can give."

A pleasant solution of the question came into Dick's mind, and he got up, beckoning mysteriously to her to come outside.

"I can exchange the needle for only one thing," he said to her on the doorstep, stammering in his effort to master her own speech. "The first day I saw you there was a string of bears' claws around your neck and an ornament at the end of it——"

"Yes, yes," she grinned and began pulling out from the folds of fur one necklace after another, elk's teeth, beads, carved nuts, ah, this was it, the claw necklace with her most beautiful jewel at the end. Joyfully she dropped the whole string into Dick's hands and received the needle in return. She was radiant with smiling gratitude as she went off down the trail, with her odd train of attendants following her, and with the pappoose bobbing and smiling at her back, its round face just showing above the buffalo robe.

"Did you sell the lady the needle?" asked Thomas Garrity when Dick came back into the cabin. "And are we to be set up in horses for the rest of our lives?"

"I sold her the needle, but not for just the price she offered," the boy replied. "You are not to know what it is for a little while."

That evening when Thomas Garrity went out with Cormac to attend to the sheep, Dick was very busy in the cabin, first with the clean sand they used to scour the copper pots, and then with a hammer and nails from the tool chest in the corner. He sat on the stool by the fire, waiting for Thomas Garrity's return, and chuckling to himself, feeling sure that the moonlight was so bright that his comrade could not miss seeing the surprise he had made ready for him. Nor was he disappointed.

"What is this?" cried Thomas Garrity, as he came in. "Sure, the little green man must have been here and nailed a horseshoe over our door. Where did you find a horseshoe, lad?"

"I bought it," returned Dick. "The Indian lady loved it I do believe, as much as the Queen loves her crown jewels, but she was willing enough to sell it for a needle."

A BARGAIN IN GOOD LUCK 201

"But you have wanted a horse this long time," urged Thomas Garrity.

Dick had said very little of his great wish; he did not know how Thomas Garrity had guessed it.

"Yes," he agreed wistfully, "and the gray mustang she brought was a sound, sturdy one. He would have been of good use to both of us, but there is only one horse in the herd that I really want, a brown one with white feet. He lets me pat his nose now every time I walk through the meadow, and he can run like the wind. Next to Mateo's black pony, he is the best one of the whole band. Do you wish I had taken the gray mustang?"

Thomas Garrity only smiled without answering.

"Only last month," Dick went on, more than half to himself, "I saw one man in the village offer a pony to another for the tail feather of an eagle." He sighed again. "I would even have liked the old mare, half a horse, she called her. But who could honorably buy a horse with a needle?"

CHAPTER XIV

THE NIGHT WATCHERS

EVEN if Dick had been the master of the beloved brown horse with white feet, he would now have had small use for him, since the snow lay so deep in the valley that no one could move about except on snowshoes. Katequa had made him a pair, slender, light ones, and beautifully curved. It required very little practice to learn to use them, so that he could soon tramp easily the length and width of the valley where otherwise he would have sunk to his knees or his waist or even his armpits in the high-piled drifts of snow.

He trampled down a wide path leading to the river, packing the soft snow firmly so that the sheep could go down to drink. It was hard work to keep breaking the ice which froze so thick every night, but with stones and a heavy pole he hammered it out every day and kept a small pool open for the thirsty sheep.

He had noticed that the wise Indian ponies knew

how to crack the ice with their pawing hoofs, and, though he had no high opinion of the intelligence of sheep, he thought that at least the ram might be taught to do the same. The big, awkward beast, however, seemed to have small gratitude for Dick's efforts to educate him, and not only did not learn, but finally lost patience and butted his master into a snowdrift, where they floundered together, the ram sunk up to his shoulders, Dick sprawling head foremost with the snowshoes uppermost, and Cormac, barking with delight and excitement, dancing up and down on the hard trail, too wise to plunge into the soft snow where the other two struggled together.

More than once Dick had brought down a deer by long following of the thin, daintily marked trail across the white hillside, had cut up the meat where it lay, and carried it and the hide home on his back. Once when the fat buck offered too heavy a load for one trip, he returned for another and found the bones already picked clean by wolves. As Mateo warned him, hunger was making the gaunt, gray beasts more and more venturesome, so that every night they howled nearer and nearer to the cabin.

At first he found opportunity to go fairly often to the Indian village to see Mateo, who lay long on the couch of deerskins in his lodge, badly wounded by the stabbing Sioux knife. The crowded, smoky dwelling was no very comfortable or cheerful place in bitter weather, nor was there much chance for those long talks of all things in heaven and earth that had been so pleasant as they sat together on the bluff above the river through the mild autumn days.

One of the things that seemed to give Mateo the most pleasure was to have Dick take out his silver sixpence and give it to his friend, who had often before looked at it and admired it. Now he would toss and juggle with it idly, slipping it from one thin hand to the other, as it shone in the wavering firelight. The Indian boy seemed to find a fascination in the smooth bit of polished metal, and he liked to hear the story of it over and over again, although the tale dealt with places and things of which he knew so little. Many times Dick tried to persuade him to keep it for his own, but Mateo always refused.

"Some harm might come to you if you gave it up," he insisted. "If it is to bring you good fortune, you must keep it always."

Even when they had an hour of private speech, it was a matter of great wonder to Dick to see how little his friend said of the attack on the camp. He spoke of the affair only once.

"It was no victory to boast of; it was only by chance that we were not all butchered in our lodges," he declared once, with brief bitterness. "Our warriors are ashamed now that they were so secure and would not keep watch. So they do not talk of the matter. Not even the one who chanced to hear the Sioux and who gave the alarm has ever told of it, so we do not know now who it was. We are all to blame."

"But you had watched all the night before," objected Dick. "You had a right to be asleep."

"A real warrior should be like a deer," Mateo insisted. "He should always be aware of his enemy's approach, even in his sleep. We had no right to be safe after such carelessness, and it was undeserved good fortune that the horses had strayed into the willows and so were not driven away."

Since he said no more, it was plain that he did not like to talk of that wild night of fighting among the lodges, so that Dick never spoke of it again. He was quite content that no one should know of his share in the affair, for, as Thomas Garrity said, he had, on that night, been where he had no business to be.

The problem of how to keep the sheep safe from the ever-threatening wolves finally drove out all other thoughts. It was plainly only a matter of time before famine should drive the hungry marauders to forget their natural fears and to come boldly up to attack the sheep pen. And as the cold grew more and more severe, after the snow had frozen hard so that light-footed beasts could run about on it without breaking through, the danger to the flock grew to be a deadly one.

Thomas Garrity shot the first wolf when it had come cowering and skulking in the shadows up to the very walls of the pen. After that, they went out almost every hour during the night to see if the danger threatened again, while Cormac, who never seemed to sleep at all, was an eager sentinel to give warning when the enemy came close.

Yet in spite of their vigilance, they lost a sheep, a lank, overgrown yearling. It slipped out through the gate of the pen in the early evening when Dick was getting the flock settled for the night. Impatient of too much confinement, it went frisking away over the hard snow and then, with one terror-stricken bleat, it went down before the onslaught of three snapping wolves that came leaping across the open slope from the woods above. Even Dick's rifle, which killed the first of the murderers at a single shot, could scarcely drive away the fighting, snarling group that gathered instantly about the dead sheep lying on the snow. Dick could hear them rustling among the bushes and pattering across the hard crust, as, having finally driven them back, he went out with Cormac to drag the poor sheep back to the pen. It had been killed instantly, and the

THE NIGHT WATCHERS 207

taste of its blood had, he knew, only whetted the sharp hunger of the savage beasts for more of its kind.

It was now plainly necessary for one of them to keep guard all night, while the other did the tasks of the day. It meant heavy labor, for up to that time it had taken the efforts of both to accomplish the toil necessary for keeping their household fed and comparatively warm. But if the sheep were to be saved, they must redouble their watchfulness, and get through the work as best they could. While Thomas Garrity slept through the day, Dick must cook the food, clean the pots and pans, and drive the sheep to the river for water and exercise. Then, whenever there was a moment to spare, he must take his axe and go out to the unending task of chopping at the tough hickory and poplar and sycamore trunks, so that the supply of firewood might never fail. Life itself depended on a sufficient fire and oh, how much wood that blazing fire could consume!

Or else, while Thomas Garrity plodded through the routine of the day, Dick watched, awake and shivering, all night long, wrapped in all the blankets and skins that their stock afforded, even to the woolly coat of the yearling lamb that the wolves had butchered. He would feed his little watch fire sparingly;

to keep warm and awake. More than once, overcome with weariness, he sat down to rest a minute and would have fallen into the frozen sleep that lasts forever had not Cormac waked him. Cormac never seemed to tire, Cormac's ears were always alert, his tail always waving, his courage and devotion always shining from his bright, expressive eyes.

"Cormac's the best man of the three of us," said Thomas Garrity once, and Dick agreed that it was so.

The French trapper had called them, "A man no longer young and a boy not yet very old," and it could not be denied that this they were. Heavy, relentless toil was not easy for a man of Thomas Garrity's age, even though he seemed still a giant in strength. And unending, dreary labor is equally hard on a growing boy who can do much in great bursts of energy, but who cannot perform a man's work, day after weary day, and not lose strength and spirit. Cormac, however, was, for a dog, in the full prime of life. He was tireless, courageous, and as excited as ever over the adventure of keeping watch each night. In Dick's estimation the shooting of wolves now had become nothing exciting, but the dreariest of labor.

The boy ached with fatigue; he had scarcely the energy to eat his daily food—monotonous fare now, since he had no longer time or strength for hunting. He wondered first whether the winter would ever end, and then grew weary even of wondering. Now indeed was the time for remembering the sailor's warning that he must always carry his courage with him. It had cost no effort to be bold in the excitement of the Sioux attack; but to keep up his spirit now, to meet each dragging day or each weary, sleepless night with a brave face—that was becoming almost beyond him. Yet he persevered. He thought of Finn McCoul with the waters of the Irish Sea rippling up to his chin, and, like the stout-hearted giant, still had courage to go forward.

He said nothing to Thomas Garrity of his weariness and discouragement, shouldered his axe cheerfully in the morning, or took up his gun at night and went forth to his work, whistling a tune which was gay enough as long as he was within hearing from the cabin, but which faltered and broke the moment he and Cormac were alone in the cold and stillness of the frozen night.

It seemed strange to have the river quiet, to hear no longer the huge, steady flowing of the Mississippi that had been such an unfailing sound in his ears through all the months of autumn. He missed it as he missed his Indian friends whom he saw so seldom now. Mateo was still lying helpless in his lodge, and Katequa could not leave him often, while Dick had so little time to go to the village that, of late, weeks had passed without their having a sight of one another.

The autumn had been long and beautiful; the winter had, in the beginning, been beautiful, too, with the sparkling white of the meadows, with the strange forms and blue shadows of the snow-buried woods, and with the blue and white of the rough, high-piled ice upon the big river. Even now, when his fatigue had grown, not only dreary, but desperate, Dick could feel vaguely, through his weariness, that it was a fair world through which he was plodding, with clean, shining days and snapping, star-lit nights. Although he did not know it, his strength was at the breaking point, but he still held up his head and faced life with as gay a spirit as he could muster.

"The wolves will be bolder than ever to-night," Thomas Garrity said one evening, as Dick made ready to go out. The older man had shot two of the gray thieves the night before. "It is cold and blowing and it is beginning to snow. Are you sure you do not want me to watch with you, lad?"

"No," Dick answered, "you need sleep as well as I do." He could hardly trust himself to say more as he pulled on his rough fur mittens and took up his rifle, so dreadfully difficult did his duty seem that night. He took up the wooden bowl that he never failed to fill, no matter how cold and weary he

THE NIGHT WATCHERS

was, and no matter how little there was to put in it. Many a small furry creature came in the dark to partake of his hospitality and to escape the starvation threatened by the unusual severity of that long winter.

"May the little green man and the horseshoe bring us luck, to-night," he said gayly, with his hand upon the door.

"I have always said Mateo was as good a friend to you as the green man could be," answered Thomas Garrity. "When you tell your grandchildren the tale of him and the bowl and the cake of wild honey, it will sound as much like a fairy story as that of the elf and your great-great-grandfather. I think it is the saints and the angels, rather than the fairies and goblins, should be with you this night."

He laid his tired head down upon the pillow of his bunk and was asleep almost before Dick had shut the door.

The snow, which had almost ceased falling, spread in a thin, diamond-powdered layer above the heavy crust that had lain unmelted for so long. Dick's feet and Cormac's made the first marks in the soft whiteness as they walked to the sheep pen and as Dick made ready his watch fire. The wind had dropped, but the sky was still covered with clouds, with never a star showing, and with all the world so silent that, as Dick stood still and listened, he could hear not a single sound. Far off, the twinkling lights of the fires about the Indian village showed him where others were watching the herd of horses as he was guarding the sheep.

He realized that he was slower and more awkward than usual as he kindled his fire, attended to the needs of the sheep, and then began to walk to and fro on his lonely sentry duty. His head dropped; his feet lagged; never had he felt such drowsiness as began to creep over him.

"If only a wolf would come," he began to wish desperately, feeling that only real danger could serve to rouse him. Last night, so Thomas Garrity said, the two wolves he had killed had crossed the open slope as familiarly as though they were dogs in their own dooryard. But nothing stirred in the underbrush; no furtive, gray shadow came stealing across the snow; there was nothing anywhere but silence and the soft whiteness of the lazily dropping flakes. An hour passed and the drowsiness became torture, then grew to be unendurable. If he could find something more to do for the sheep, he thought, perhaps it might help to keep him awake.

He opened the door of the shed, warm within from the breath of the sleeping animals, and the warmth of the woolly bodies huddled together on their bed of clean hay. As Dick stepped within, he

THE NIGHT WATCHERS 213

heard the first sound that had broken the dead stillness of the night, the crack of a rifle on the hillside above.

"Some Indian on a night hunt," he told himself hazily, "but then Indians do not often hunt at night in winter. I must see——"

A block of wood underfoot made him stumble in the dark, and he fell full length upon the straw. It was so soft and warm and such delicious peace to rest there!

"I will lie here just a minute," he thought and was almost instantly asleep. Another gunshot sounded from the hill, but did not waken him. Cormac whined and pushed him with his nose, but his weary master did not stir. The dog made more than one puzzled effort to rouse him, then, with a sigh for his own weariness, curled up against the boy in a round, warm cushion of fur and closed his own eyes. Dick had rolled against the big ram and, lying between the two, was as warm as if he had been in his bunk in the cabin. The snow ceased falling; the skies cleared and the stars came out; but still he slept on. His tired body had finally refused to follow his will; he had done all that one boy could do, and exhaustion had taken possession of him at last.

It was hours later that he awoke, felt, in bewilderment, the woolly shoulder of the ram against which he was lying, realized where he was, and sat up quickly.

"It must have been only for a few minutes," he assured himself hopefully, and got up stiffly to look out at the door. The night had turned from black to gray; his little fire was burned to cold ashes; and above the big river the sky, marked with faint rose color, showed promise of the dawn.

"It can't be morning; it can't be!" he kept repeating. What had the wolves been doing while he was asleep?

In wild haste he counted the sheep; they were all there. He pushed through the gate of the pen and, in the growing light, scanned the smooth slope of the snow. It lay in soft, unbroken white, just as it had fallen, with never a footprint in any direction. This first night that he had failed to keep watch was the first that the prowling enemies had not come near.

Thomas Garrity, waking to see Dick before the cabin fire making preparations for breakfast, asked him as he always did: "How did the night pass?"

Dick confessed bravely.

"It was so quiet and I was so tired that I went to sleep. But nothing came near, and the sheep are all there. I counted them over and over."

It was Thomas Garrity who watched the next

night and who came in at daybreak to announce wonderingly that again no wolf had come near the pen. The cold was more bitter than ever; the wolves had been howling across the hill in the early dark, but they had not broken the quiet of Thomas Garrity's watch. An unaccountable spell seemed to have fallen upon the threatened sheepfold; peace had come after the long siege of terror.

The next night, when it was Dick's time to mount guard, he curled up in the straw and slept openly, leaving Cormac to give warning should any danger come near. The morning broke, and again never a sign of a wolf's stealthy feet was left upon the snow. Thereafter, neither he nor Thomas Garrity remained awake. They took their guns and spent the nights in the sheepshed in proper turn, but so worn out were they that once the sense of danger was removed they slept like dead men and could scarcely have roused themselves had the whole pack come leaping over the wall.

Dick, being the younger, was the first to emerge from the first stages of utter weariness. There came, at last, a night when curiosity kept him awake as surely as complete exhaustion had driven him to sleep. There was some reason, he felt certain, for this curious lull in the danger that had oppressed them so long. What that reason was, he had determined to find out.

He must have watched an hour—perhaps two—when he heard, as he had heard that first night, the report of a gun in the woods above him. Peering earnestly through the dark, he saw a tiny spark of red, glowing against the snow, just where the open slope touched the edge of the forest. Leaving Cormac in charge of the sheep pen, he made his way across the hard snowfield, up the steep hill, and so to the edge of the trees. There was a tiny fire burning in the shelter of a fallen log, a fire so abundant as to heat and light, yet so sparing as to smoke and fuel, that it was surely of an Indian's making. No one was beside it at the moment, but, all about, the snow was trampled with the marks of moccasined feet. Dick sat down upon the log with his gun across his knees and waited. Presently a tall, striding figure came out of the dark, grunted an Indian greeting, and sat down on the opposite side of the fire.

Dick recognized the man at once as Haidan, the chief of the tribe, husband of Waponjea. He was past middle age, with a strong, deeply lined face, on which the red firelight shone as upon the features of a bronze statue. What could he be doing here, the boy wondered. The two sat staring at each other without speaking for some minutes.

The Indian had dragged behind him the skin of a freshly killed wolf which he had flung in a heap

THE NIGHT WATCHERS

beside the fire before he sat down. He looked at Dick steadily, yet never said a word, evidently waiting for the boy to speak first. Among so many questions that he wished to ask, Dick could scarcely make the choice or find the Indian words to state the first one.

"Why do you come up here to kill wolves when there are plenty hanging about the village, hungering for your horses as they hunger for our sheep?" he said at last.

Even then the other did not reply at once, and, when he did speak, seemed to be answering to little purpose.

"We have heard a strange story," he began. "The Sioux are our enemies, but they are friends with the Osages, and the Osages are friends with the Iowas, who are at peace with us." He paused as though to make sure that the boy, with his halting knowledge of the Indian tongue, had followed his meaning. As Dick nodded he went on.

"So a tale has come round to us, of why the Sioux failed in their attack that night. They said that a white-faced stranger stood up in the moonlight and shouted warning to the sleeping camp; they said that when they sought to drive the horses into the river, that same strange youth and a creature like a yellow wolf turned the plunging beasts into the willows.

All this news came to us slowly after three moons. And we had never known what saved us!"

Dick sat looking down at the snow at his feet, digging in it with the butt of his rifle, and since he found nothing to answer, remained silent.

"What—what else could I have done?" he asked huskily, at last.

"Since he said nothing, we said nothing," the Indian continued. "But we saw that he and his comrade were having a fierce battle against the cold and those gray robbers, the wolves; we saw both the man and the boy growing worn and anxious, yet never asking for help. In this bitter weather no man—and far less a boy—can toil and watch and spend himself forever; a night comes when he sleeps in the open in spite of the cold, in spite of everything, and never wakes. The Indians know that; but a white man does not. So we have set ourselves to watch for him, and we build our fire here every night and with gun or arrows strike down every wolf that crosses the open to steal down to the dwelling of your sheep. We have taken the skins from the wolves we have killed; the women are dressing them; and you shall some day have as many wolfskins as you have sheep. You can go back to your lodge of logs and lie down to sleep without fear, since no harm can come to you now.

THE NIGHT WATCHERS 219

Every warrior in the village has sworn that those two on the hill and all that belongs to them shall be kept safe."

So this was the meaning of the sudden peace that had followed their long battle for the safety of the sheep! Dick felt as though a great weight had fallen from his shoulders. That task—he could face the truth now—had become heavy beyond the strength of one man and one boy, but it was now to be shared by a score of able friends. He stretched his feet to the warmth of the fire and smiled up at his companion.

"I think I will not go back to sleep in the cabin to-night," he said. "I will watch here with you."

So the two sat, on opposite sides of the fire, sometimes talking, sometimes silent for long spaces of time. Dick heard that Mateo was better and soon could walk forth again, that he was esteemed a warrior now, since he had taken such valiant part in the battle with the Sioux. He learned that the winter had been a harder one than usual, that the supply of dried buffalo meat was low in the lodges, and that everyone was longing for the cold to break and the spring hunting to begin.

"Will the cold ever end?" Dick asked desperately. "I begin to think winter lasts half the year here by the Mississippi!"

"It will end some day," replied the other, and added suddenly: "Hush." He held up his hand. "Hush and listen."

While they had talked, the wall of blackness about them had turned to gray, the sky had grown bright to the eastward, and morning had come. In the top of a tall, bare tree at the edge of the forest a bird was swinging. It was a brilliantly red bird that Dick had seen from time to time flitting about the bushes and dry weeds, looking like a glowing coal with his bright-colored coat against the snow. He had never known him to give forth any sound other than a half-frozen chirp, but now, as the Indian bade him listen, he heard the bird begin to sing. He trilled, he whistled, he balanced on his twig, raised his crest, swelled out his throat, and sang until it seemed the whole white, sleeping valley must awake and hear him.

"Birds are wiser than men," said the Indian, "and there, so far above the frozen earth, that bird can feel the spring."

Thomas Garrity, suddenly awakened by Dick's excited homecoming, could scarcely believe the tale that the boy poured out.

"We need not watch any longer," Dick kept saying, "we can sleep and sleep and sleep. Even Cormac can rest. The sheep are safe and the spring is coming!"

CHAPTER XV

THE EAGLE DANCE

IN spite of the prophecy of the cardinal-coated bird, the cold still refused to relax its last hold upon the frozen earth. Every day, however, the sun seemed to shine longer and brighter, the huge-piled drifts began to shrink and crumble, and the bowed trees dropped their heavy white load and stood erect again. The little watch fire on the hill above them never failed, so that now, when Dick had bedded the sheep for the night, he could look up at its friendly red eye peering through the dark, could close the door of the cabin, and sleep without care until morning. Sometimes, before he went in, he would climb the steep slope and sit for a little while with the guardian of the night: sometimes it was with Haidan, the chief; sometimes with Machetawan, the old hunter, who knew more of the lore of the wild things in the woods, of the signs of weather in the clouds and in the color of the river and in the shadows on the prairie, than any other man. Or he would spend an hour of talk with one or another of the younger braves, who were all desperately impatient for the cold to break and the summer's hunting to be at hand once more.

One evening as he came up the hill a smaller, slimmer figure sat upon the log by the fire, one which he had not seen there before, but which was familiar none the less.

"Mateo!" he cried out joyfully, and Mateo it was, thin from illness, and still limping, but well on the way to recovery. Far into the night Dick sat with him, while the two talked together, often both at once, since there was so much for each to tell the other.

"We are waiting only to hear the voice of the river again," Mateo told him, "and then the whole camp will fall to work to clean and oil the guns and dress the arrows for the buffalo hunting."

"I did not think such great animals could be killed by arrows," Dick said.

"Guns are good for deer and for birds," the Indian boy answered, "but most of us still think that arrows are better for the buffalo. When you are galloping headlong after one of the big beasts and have wounded him and he turns upon you, then the white man's gun is long and awkward to reload, but the friendly arrow is always ready to your hand. We none of us think or talk of anything now but what it would be to be hunting on the prairie again, to be riding in a choking cloud of dust with the

THE EAGLE DANCE 223

horses wheeling and dodging and the great, black buffalo falling on every side. As soon as the grass is green and the horses are fat once more, our lodges will come down and our goods will be packed and we will be off."

Both fell silent after these words, for neither, perhaps, had realized until that moment that the spring would mean the parting of two good friends.

"Could you—could you never live the whole year around in the valley?" asked Dick.

"There is not game enough left in these hills to keep us alive," Mateo said. "Once, long ago, in a time that our fathers' grandfathers scarcely remember, our people lived far to the north, in pine forests and on the shores of great stormy lakes. But they drifted and drifted, driven by enemies and following the game, until they came to the Mississippi. Here we have lived so long now that the love for that blue, running water and for the high, green bluffs has become a part of our very bones and sinews. Yet, we all know that some day we may have to go on once more."

"But men can live by plowing and planting," Dick urged. "You can grow enough corn and melons and beans in these green meadows for a far bigger tribe than yours."

But to this Mateo could not agree.

"An Indian is a hunter," he said simply. "He

may learn to live by planting the earth, as an eagle may learn to live in a cage, but it will take more years than you and I shall ever see, to teach him to do so."

It was hard on midnight when Dick at last left his friend and returned to the cabin. The snow no longer squeaked under his feet, for the cold had diminished little by little, until now it was scarcely freezing. In the morning he awoke to see water pouring from the edge of the roof where the white covering had at last begun to melt. Outside in the brilliant sunshine the whole hillside was swimming with the icy streams that went trickling in every direction down the slope. The sheep splashed as they walked, and Cormac, dashing about in circles in a riot of joy that the winter had broken, sent out fountains of sparkling drops from under his splattering feet. Three nights later Dick awoke suddenly with the knowledge that something had happened. What was it? What had he heard so insistently through his dreams, that it had brought him forcibly to wakefulness? Beyond the bluff he heard a strange noise of crashing and grinding and through it a huge, subdued roar, as of great, impatient waters running free at last. It was the voice of the river!

In the morning Katequa and Mateo came up the trail to stand with him on the summit of the bluff above the Mississippi and to watch the ever-widen-

THE EAGLE DANCE 225

ing spaces of blue water. The rotten, gray ice, furrowed with white where the floating cakes had rubbed and ground together, sailed away down the current or piled itself up along the shore. Below them, on the other side of the high point of land, the Des Moines was flowing with swift, dancing water, then plunging under the ice again, splashing and chafing along the shores.

"The warriors will be dancing the Eagle Dance about the fires to-night," said Katequa, "and presently Haidan will send a messenger to bid you and your comrade come to watch it."

At noontime the messenger arrived with due ceremony, a long-legged young brave, who came striding up the hill, clattering with all the metallic ornaments and gay decorations of an Indian warrior's full magnificence. He shouted a greeting before the door and then came in, stooping his tall, feather-decked head under the door frame. He repeated with great ceremony the message of Haidan, that both his white friends were begged to be present when the Eagle Dance was performed. Every year, he explained, it was danced in honor of the new season of warmth and plenty and hunting of the buffalo again. The place of the dance was to be the hillside at the edge of the forest, where the men of the tribe had watched for wolves through the cold winter nights.

Dick translated the stately words of the chief's

message to Thomas Garrity, and attempted to put their reply into equally dignified Indian speech. Whether he succeeded in doing so was a doubtful matter, but the other accepted his answer with the same ceremonious manner and went striding and clattering away again.

When the dusk had fallen and when the two could see the bright bonfires blazing in a circle against the dark of the tree trunks, Dick and Thomas Garrity made their way up the hill. The boy was never to forget that scene, the leaping light of the fires, the myriad moving figures, the strange-shaped dancing shadows that seemed to multiply the numbers of the throng. The women and children were gathered in one group beside the biggest fire, where they sat with drums of bull hide between their knees. Katequa looked up and smiled at Dick as they passed, but she said no word, for this was the festival of the warriors and hunters, not of the women.

Mateo came presently, threading his way through the crowd, to say that Haidan wished for a word with Thomas Garrity under the great oak tree at the edge of the wood. It was a long word, apparently. Dick could look across the blazing circle and see them, first smoking a pipe together and then, through the Indian boy, plunged into earnest talk. He wondered at their lengthy consultation and at their not asking for his presence as interpreter.

THE EAGLE DANCE 227

"Perhaps they always talk a long time when they are smoking peace pipes," he thought vaguely, too absorbed in the scene before him to pay much attention to the matter.

He loved watching the tall warriors stalking back and forth in the firelight and wearing strange head-dresses, some made from buffalo horns, some from the dyed and bristling hair of deers' tails, some from black and white eagle feathers. Strings of agate beads and bright feathers hung also from their shields, their bows, and their painted war clubs, and swung about their legs as they walked. It was beautiful to see the smooth play of the easy muscles under the red skin, to watch the firelight illuminate their earnest, clean-cut faces and glittering black eyes.

At last Thomas Garrity came back to sit down beside him.

"What was the chief telling you all this long time?" Dick asked, but before Thomas Garrity could answer there was a sudden absolute silence; one slow drum began to thump, and then another; and the dance began.

At the center of the circular space, inside the ring of fire, four tall lances, bright with painted shafts and colored streamers, had been set upright in the hard earth. One warrior after another, beginning with the eldest, came forward and, crouching almost to the ground, danced in and out among the four spears, swinging his war club around his head, sounding his whirling rattle, and then spreading out his arms to imitate the hovering wings of the eagle. In every motion he kept time to the pounding of the drums and the shrill ah—ah—ah of the chanting women. When he had finished his dance, he stood up and with signs and gestures told of some spirited deed of fighting or hunting taken from his past experience. There seemed no element of boasting in each one's telling of what he had done. It was only thus that a record of the history of the tribe could be kept. Those younger braves who had performed no stirring deed of their own, told of something in the record of their fathers or grandfathers. There was a savage grace and dignity in each lean, red figure, as one after another came forward, went through the dance in the weird changing firelight and slipped back into his place. Last of all it was Mateo's turn.

Dick, glancing across to the largest fire and to where Katequa sat, saw her grow intent, watched her beat her drum with new energy, and thought that he could almost see her eyes flash with pride as her brother danced his crouching way among the lances and then stood up to tell his unspoken tale. So intent was he on watching his two friends that Dick was quite unconscious that every Indian now leaned for-

THE EAGLE DANCE 229

ward, that the drumming and singing dropped to a murmur and that all eyes went slowly from Mateo to himself.

With his thin straight figure showing black against the brilliant fire, the Indian boy went through a new and elaborate pantomime setting forth a story so graphically that there was scarcely need for words. He showed a crouching enemy stealing up a hill through the underbrush; then showed an unconscious passer-by who suddenly became aware of the enemy's presence and dropped to cover, waiting in tense expectancy for his adversary to move. It was only when the narrative had reached this point that Dick realized with a shock of surprise and of something like consternation that the tale had to do with himself.

The whole course of the events of that stirring night was set forth: the wild plunge down the hillside, the dash along the frozen river, the cry of warning that finally aroused the village. Then was pictured the attempt to drive the horses into the stream and the desperate efforts of Dick and Cormac to turn them aside from destruction. Last of all was shown a single, weary figure, turning away from the scene of the struggle, and toiling painfully back to the cabin on the hill.

The fires had died down in the progress of the dance, and had fallen lower still during Mateo's final share in it; so that only one, the largest, was now left burning to light his last sweeping gesture as he stepped back from his place. There was no shrill chorus of applause from the women, such as had followed the other dancers; there was, instead, complete silence, as even the thumping of the drums ceased. Out of the dark beyond the fire came Haidan, leading two ponies, both decked out with the bright-colored trappings of an Indian chieftain's war horse. One was the stout, gray mustang that Waponjea had brought to the cabin; the other, with arched neck and light, daintily stepping white feet, was the brown horse of Dick's long desire.

Partly because Thomas Garrity pushed at his arm, partly in response to a motion from the chief's hand, the boy got up and went forward. Even in the waning firelight he made a strange contrast to the dark, sinewy figures about him; he was so much shorter and more squarely built, the blue of his eyes and the fairness of his skin showed so plainly, even in the fitful glare of the dying flames. The chief put the two rawhide bridles into his hand. Dick took them, marveling, feeling an agony of pleasure and embarrassment, wondering desperately what he ought to say.

He might have spared himself that desperate question, for the moment his hand had touched the bridles, the ceremony was at an end. No word was

THE EAGLE DANCE 231

spoken; scarcely even a whisper or a footstep was to be heard, as some one scattered and quenched the brands of the fire, while the whole company slipped away into the darkness. There is nothing so silent as an Indian, and a hundred Indians can be as still as a single one. They might have been the Little People themselves from the fashion in which they vanished into the shadows, leaving Dick standing between the two horses, with the brown pony's soft nose rubbing against his cheek.

CHAPTER XVI.

THE BLOOM OF THE YEAR

SPRING came in at last, with the exciting rush that surprises mankind all over again every year. The ice was gone, and the meadows were growing green along the edge of the river before the snow wreaths had vanished at the edge of the forest. The ducks and geese were flying overhead again, and the whole world seemed to be full of fluttering wings, of restlessness, and the stir of coming change.

The autumn had been a busy season; the winter had been a laborious one; and now the spring seemed to bring the most pressing work of all. The flock of sheep was larger by more than a third than it had been in the autumn and required three times as much care. Numerous small, wobbly-legged lambs trotted about on the meadows, which were growing daily deeper in new grass. There was, moreover, the shearing of the sheep to be accomplished, a task almost impossible for only two pairs of hands.

Here, however, Dick and Thomas Garrity received unexpected assistance, for several of the Indian braves came up the hill to help them. Dick was far more awkward with the big sheep shears than were any of these warriors whose hands were deft, and whose steel muscles never seemed to tire. To cut away the wool of these strange, new animals was so nearly akin to skinning a deer or an antelope that the red hunters considered it a man's work, and learned to handle the shears as easily and carefully as Thomas Garrity himself. The work was brought successfully to an end without injury to a single sheep, and the assistants went away delighted with the gifts they had received in return for their labor, two knives, a red blanket, and a copper saucepan.

It was amazing to see the bulk of the great bundles of wool which were piled up on the floor of the cabin, and to calculate what price they would bring even in the frontier market of St. Louis, whither they were to be sent.

Dick and Thomas Garrity sat late together on the doorstone, resting after the labor of counting the bundles and tying them into bales. It was a soft, delicious night, with the sweetness of the wild hawthorn, now in full bloom along the hills, coming down to them in scented waves on the warm wind. The hedges would be blooming in Ireland now, and the same fragrance would be drifting past the tiny cottage that Dick had left so far behind. The sailor would be smoking his solitary pipe on the bench below the eaves, and the blue-white star, that stood above their chimney now, that had hung above the mast head when he had crossed the seas, would be shining at this moment above the cottage at home. It was a year since Dick had set out, a year of such far journeying and of such changing adventure that it seemed more like half a lifetime.

"You know," said Thomas Garrity, looking strangely idle as he sat resting at last, with his big hands upon his knees, "you know that soon those boatmen who brought us here will be returning with new supplies for the summer, with seeds and a plow to turn up that fat, black land in the meadows yonder. Do you think that we, between us, can break the gray mustang to the task of plowing? It is something that no Indian horse has ever learned to do."

"I think we can," assented Dick. "And will the men take our wool back to be sold in St. Louis?"

"Yes," replied Thomas Garrity; "I arranged with a merchant there to take it for us and to buy in our behalf whatever we send him word that we need. And you must not forget that half of what we receive for the wool is yours."

"No, no," Dick objected quickly. "Why should it be?"

"The ram is yours, and the dog, and they are the two chief things in a venture of sheep raising. If

THE BLOOM OF THE YEAR

you do not think that you yourself are worthy to be an equal partner in this affair, you must admit that Cormac is. And such hard work as you have expended, with so little complaint! Has your heart gone back to Ireland in this past year? Have you wished that you were at home again and had never seen the new world or Thomas Garrity?"

"Never!" Dick returned with vehemence. Since that last agony of homesickness on shipboard, when he had finally gathered up his courage to see the venture through, he had never once felt any real wish to go back. Some day—he had thought of it long, and now, with the news that he was really a partner with Thomas Garrity, he could count on it more certainly—some day he would send for Bridget Anne and Michael to come and be their neighbors here on the green hillside above the river. Among the wolfskins that Haidan had given him, at the end of the season of watching on the hill, was a soft, silky, white one. This, so he planned in his heart, he would contrive to send to the shy little girl, John Brogan's daughter, who had begged her father to give him Cormac, and who had wished him good fortune as he ran down the lane. What good fortune he had found; what friends he had made; what a full and wonderful year it had been!

"We shall not even be equal partners for long," went on Thomas Garrity, whose thoughts had evidently not wandered so far across the world as had Dick's. "With every year that goes by, you will be able to do more, and I to do less; so that it will be no great time before you are the real man of this undertaking. And even now the true success of the affair lies with you."

In reply to Dick's exclamation of surprise and disbelief, he went on to make a more complete explanation. As they sat talking, Cormac came through the dark and lay down beside his master with a weary thump, a tired, yet well-satisfied dog. He had been on a careful tour of inspection, since the safety of all the young lambs seemed to weigh heavily upon his mind. The wolves had drifted away across the hills long since, seeking some more familiar quarry; but those woolly, bleating babies were such tempting morsels that Cormac, even now, appeared to feel that he could not be too watchful.

"Although we did not know it," Thomas Garrity was saying, "we had chosen unwisely when we took just this place for our dwelling. The Government of this country has lately made a new treaty with the Sac-and-Fox tribe, whereby the Indians gave up all their lands east of the Mississippi, and moved to this side of it, where the country was not to be open to settlement. No white man was to dwell on this ground except, as was most unlikely, by the particular wish and friendship of the Indians. I did not

THE BLOOM OF THE YEAR

learn this until after the cabin was built; I was told of it by Gil Surette. It was too late then to move away, although the Indians would have been within their rights had they driven us from the place and burned our cabin. It was the growing friendship between you and Mateo that gave me hope of its being safe for us to remain."

Dick had puzzled for long over that chance remark of Gil Surette's, that the success of the affair lay with him; but he had finally put it from his mind, as a problem that he could not solve. And now he was to understand it at last.

"On that night of the Eagle Dance, the chief, Haidan, talked to me of the same thing," Thomas Garrity went on. "There is one branch of their tribe, living to the northward, and led by the fierce young chief called Black-Hawk, who has vowed that white men and Indians shall never dwell together, and who has often counselled Haidan to drive us from the valley. But Haidan has watched you and Mateo as I have, and he has seen how much may pass between a white boy and an Indian to the benefit of both. He says that the Sac-and-Fox village is proud of its white neighbors, and he has pledged me his word that he and every chief after him will let us abide in peace."

"But—but why did you never tell me?" questioned Dick.

"I could not tell you, for no friendship is of any worth that is poisoned by the thought of what can be gained by it. Even Gil Surette was too fair to tell you—I honor him for that. But the French trapper said other things in his effort to make me join him, things that I have remembered long. He said that you would never be content with a hard, bitter man like me, that for the sake of your happiness I should persuade you to go with him. Has it been so hard, lad, to spend all these long, lonely months with a harsh, sour fellow like Thomas Garrity?"

"Oh, no, no," cried Dick. "How could you think so? How could Gil Surette say such wicked things?"

They did not yet know that the French trapper was dead; they thought of him still as he had last stood in the cabin, alive and eager, smiling his crafty, wolfish smile. It was agony to Dick to think that what the man had said should have hurt and troubled Thomas Garrity for so long. Yet even now he could not completely break down the reserve that stood between them; he could think of nothing to say or do that would comfort and reassure his friend. But Cormac, unlike these two clumsy humans, was quite untroubled by the fear of showing what was really in his heart, and jumped up to overwhelm Thomas Garrity with licks and rough caresses. He had heard pain in the tone of his voice and in Dick's

THE BLOOM OF THE YEAR

distressed reply, and he sought, by means of every doggish endearment that he knew, to make both of his masters happy again.

A question which had long been forming in Dick's mind now found voice at last.

"Have you been homesick for Ireland?" he asked.

"Not—not in the way that you might think," his comrade returned, after pondering a little. "For a man as old as I am, it is hard to forget a place and a life, once so much loved, even after that love has broken off in bitterness. But I love this place, too; I have the feeling, which I think you have also, that we and this green valley have grown to be one; that we belong to it, rather than that it belongs to us."

Dick nodded. It was, in truth, just what he felt.

"It is so the Indians feel," Thomas Garrity continued, "and it is what every settler on the frontier should learn to understand. If you had looked for the making of much money in this venture, if you had been one of those who wishes to grasp as many acres of land as he can, and sell them again, this would be no place for you. The man who looks only for money and adventure must come and go again, and leave nothing behind him. Unless you have felt your blood quicken at the sight of the autumn color spreading over the hills, or at the blue of that great river rolling down to the sea; unless you have wished, not to possess this new country, but to be a part of it, then you are no true pioneer, and you will never succeed. The wilderness will have none of you!"

Dick's arm, which was around Cormac, drew suddenly tight, as he moved closer against Thomas Garrity's knee. These three together should surely prosper in the wilderness, if a love for it and for each other could bring prosperity. He thought, all at once, of Anthony Robins with his wide, black hat and flapping, long-waisted coat, and his bitter comment on his own adventure on the frontier— "I sold out for scarcely twice what I put in, and I lost a whole year of my life while I was doing it."

Such a year as they had spent was the sort of year that Anthony Robins had lost. Had he left the new country in the spring, at a season like this, with the pink crabapple in bloom among the white hawthorn, with the woods cool and dark and carpeted with flowers? Had he last seen some tumbling western river, rising beyond its banks as the Des Moines had done, singing over its rapids and shining with an intricate pattern of shifting light? Had he gone stumping back to civilization with his coat tails flapping and his hardly won profits jingling in his pockets? He laughed out loud at the thought of it.

"What is it?" asked Thomas Garrity, startled out of a reverie of his own.

THE BLOOM OF THE YEAR 241

"I was laughing at Anthony Robins," Dick told him, and Thomas Garrity seemed to see, in his own imagination, something of the same picture, for he laughed, also, as he got up to go in.

"It is dark to-night," he said, looking about the wide circle of the sky, "but to-morrow, unless I have miscounted the days, there will be a new moon. Come in, lad, the night is for sleeping dreams, not waking ones."

Through all the next day, Dick, as he looked toward the village, could see, even from that distance, that the last preparations for departure were going forward. He did not like to go near, feeling that he would be in the way where the final tasks were being performed, feeling, also, a heart so heavy over the going of his friends that he preferred to be alone. Did Indians say good-by when they set out on a journey? He did not know, and spent the whole of the day wondering whether he was to see Mateo and Katequa again.

It rained at the end of the afternoon, in a fresh, spring shower that splashed upon the grass and pattered on the leaves for half an hour. Then it ceased, leaving the spring world greener and gayer even than before. In the misery of his restless loneliness, Dick had wandered down the hill to the edge of the Des Moines, and, when the shower came up, had sat down under the shelter of a spreading thorn tree, whose white blossoms dropped all about him under the soft beating of the rain. When the spattering drops had almost ceased and the sun had come out again, he still sat, with his chin leaning on his hand, and his heart still heavy with the knowledge of how he would miss his friends through the long summer season. His thoughts went wandering farther and farther away, half noticing the beauty of the world about him, half carrying the sense of that beauty far off into the distant regions whither his roaming fancy had traveled.

There were wild roses coming out everywhere among the close-growing bushes near the river, wet and sweet-smelling roses, unfolding their crumpled petals under the warm rain. Not even the Bendemeer's stream of Thomas Garrity's song could be fairer, so he thought, than the rushing river that ran at his feet, with its green banks, its blossoming thickets, and with the rising hills of its valley covered with drifts of white and pink and pale, quivering green. The straight lines of the falling rain had caught the sun; so that the arch of a rainbow stood high and glittering just over the green islands where the little Des Moines widened to meet the stately, blue Mississippi. As though in answer to the brightening sunshine and in spite of the thin,

THE BLOOM OF THE YEAR

sparkling raindrops, a bird in the nearest thicket began to sing.

He was a bird of about the size of the yellow-billed blackbird who used to sing in the hedge at home. He had a coat of black and white like a magpie, with a splash of rose-red on his breast. Dick and Thomas Garrity had heard him sing before, and Thomas Garrity had said that his voice "was like an angel's, done very small."

There was indeed something very like an angel's singing in the bird's notes, so joyous were they, so round and full and silvery. Rainbows, also, had always made Dick think of angels and archangels, such as Bridget Anne used to describe, of the cherubim with golden helmets and the seraphim with flaming swords. He tried to think of how the bird's voice would sound, a hundred times bigger, filling the whole sky with the joyful chorus of an angel choir. He wished that he could tell Mateo and Katequa of all that the blossoming valley and the bird and the rainbow had made him think of—but no, it would take a long, long time to make them understand about angels. And he had forgotten that they were going away, that those talks by the river had come to an end.

Not quite to an end, even yet. As he sat there, he heard footsteps, and saw the brother and sister coming along the bank of the stream, walking side by side without a word. They had come as much to bid farewell to the river and the meadows and the whole green valley as to say good-by to him. That was evident in the hungry way that their eyes went over every loved portion of this corner of the blossoming spring world that belonged to them. The Indian boy and girl had little knowledge of such a thing as owning land, they would as easily have thought they could fence off a square of the blue sky and call it theirs, but they had something which no mere possession of broad acres could ever give, a feeling that their lives and their happiness were bound up in every twist of the singing river, in every curve of the wooded hills.

Katequa smiled as she saw Dick under the thorn tree, but Mateo's intent face did not relax as the two came and sat down, without a word, on the grass beside their friend. The rainbow was fading; the rain had practically ceased; and the sun was dropping to the horizon. The bird, at their coming, had flown away.

It seemed that the three had no need of speech or sign as they sat together, watching the shining day come to an end and saying good-by in silence.

"Come with us," Mateo broke out at last. "You love to hunt and to ride; you would be as happy as we on the wide prairies with the rippling grass

THE BLOOM OF THE YEAR

and the racing shadows of clouds and the sunshine everywhere."

"Couldn't you?" pleaded Katequa, "couldn't you? Your comrade could do without you for a little; it would be a glorious summer; it would be so good to come home again!"

Of all the times that he had been asked to turn aside from his chosen way, this was the moment when it was most difficult to refuse. Dick could not bear to answer; he could only shake his head. There were certain things about the Indian life, certain dark, cruel secrets of their endless warfare among themselves, that would forever bar him from falling in completely with their ways of living. But how much these two had taught him, not only of how to hunt and fish and live in the wilderness, but also of loyalty, of friendship, of unquestioning and unspeaking courage!

Neither of the two pressed the question of his coming with them; they seemed to have known beforehand that his answer must be no. Mateo laid down a bundle that he had been carrying under his arm, which, on being unrolled, proved to be the soft hide of a cow buffalo. It had been rubbed with white clay until the inner surface was as smooth and fair as paper. He and Katequa, searching busily, found enough dry sticks and leaves to make a little fire. Mateo worked long over his fire-sticks to kindle the tiny blaze in the wet grass; the fuel caught at last and sent forth a drift of blue smoke, that floated lazily away across the surface of the river.

"The Sioux are hunting to the northward this season, so we hear," Mateo said, as he nursed the first small flame between his hands. "So, unless the buffalo are very few, we will have no quarrels with our enemies for a little."

"Has there always been war between the Sioux and the Sac-and-Fox tribe?" asked Dick.

"No, once we were at peace with them, when the buffalo were plenty and there was abundant hunting for all. But the buffalo grew fewer, and we began to see that some time there will not be enough for both tribes. Since then there has been war."

"But what will you do as the buffalo grow less and less? How will you live?" Dick questioned.

"We will go farther and farther west, and some day we will never come back."

The fire was crackling now, and the larger sticks were fairly ablaze. The sun was gone; the light in the sky was dull gold; the hills had grown dark; and above them rode the thin, silver crescent of the new moon. The water of the big river was silver gray beyond the islands, and its deep voice sounded louder and louder up the valley as the twilight darkened.

THE BLOOM OF THE YEAR 247

Mateo had taken up one of the burning sticks from the fire and with its glowing end was making strange black marks on the white of the buffalo hide. Katequa kept handing him new firebrands as the old ones cooled, and watched his task intently, without a word. First he made, in the corner, a curious drawing which Dick recognized as the mark of the Sac-and-Fox tribe, a winding river running obliquely, with a rudely pictured fox at each end. Then, on the main surface of the hide he began to draw a map of the valley. Here was the Des Moines River with its thickets and willows; here was the Mississippi with heavy dark lines burnt into the leather to denote the wooded bluffs. Here at a bend in the smaller stream were pointed lodges to denote the Indian village; here were the marks of moccasins to stand for the trail across the meadows. Here was the cabin and here, quaintly pictured, were the sheep upon the hillside.

"Haidan has told you that you shall always live at peace here in our valley, and that the next chief after him shall promise you the same thing. But I have thought that a time will come when Haidan is dead, when the next chief is dead—whether it be myself or some other—when you and those who come after you may need to show that you have had that promise. So here is a picture of the lands where you and your white friends may abide forever.

Here, even in those days when we have gone too far away to return, you will still have proof that it is by the love and desire of the Indians that such white men as you should live here after them. I have the right to give you this, since I am the son of a chief."

He made a crooked mark in the lower corner, like a stroke of lightning coming from a cloud.

"That is to stand for my name," he said, "the title they give me now that I am a warrior, Companion of the Thunder."

Katequa took the brand and made in her turn the picture of a flying bird to stand for her name, the Eagle's Maiden. She handed the glowing stick to Dick, who wrote his name below in round, rude characters, Dick Martin. Then this rude document, proving his right to a home in the wilderness, was rolled up and laid across his knees.

The two Indians stood up, and Katequa slipped away into the dark.

"Wait," said Dick to Mateo, who would have followed her.

He brought from his pocket the silver sixpence, laid it upon a stone, and, by hammering away at it with the point of his knife, finally managed to separate it into two jagged halves. As he worked, his mind went back to the night he had found it in the garden, and to the evening of the new moon when he had wished on it, had fallen over the cliff, and so had met the sailor on the sands below. How far reaching had been their talk together, there where the waves came splashing in! It had carried him across the seas and it had brought to him— Dick could only tell vaguely, even within himself, the sum of what he had gained in adventure, friendship, and happy living. It had brought him all this. It had shown him how to have courage through the hard places of the way. And his knowledge of the sailor had taught him one more thing, which he had only realized completely at this moment.

"It's sixpences that are the coin of life, not sovereigns nor gold doubloons nor Spanish pieces-of-eight, but jingling, silver sixpences. It's the little coins and the little minutes that make a life happy in the end."

It would be hard for him to forget some of his adventures, in particular that great hour by the river on the night of the Sioux attack, but what he would remember even longer, he now knew, were some of the quieter, but completely happy moments—that evening on shipboard when Thomas Garrity was singing, those golden autumn afternoons on the bluff by the river, talking with Mateo, that night by the fire in the cold and snow with Haidan, this last hour with his truest friend in the gathering shadows with the new moon above them.

He had finished dividing the sixpence at last.

"Will you keep one half, if I keep the other?" he asked.

Mateo nodded and took the half of the broken coin. He stood for a moment, saying no word, then swung on his heel and vanished without a sound into the dusk. Dick was quite content; he, too, had no need for words of farewell. He sat beside the fire with his arms about his knees, thinking still of sailors and new moons, of beloved friends and silver sixpences.

In the morning, he and Cormac stood upon the hillside at dawn and watched the Indians take their slow way out of the valley. Horses, and warriors, women, children, and dogs, in a long line they wound across the meadows, up the far slope of the bluff, and out of sight. In his mind's eye he could follow them across the dewy grass of the flat prairie, in a black twisting line, to disappear over the edge of the horizon.

They would come back, once, twice, how many times? But some day, in just that silent fashion, they would journey away to the westward and never return. And it seemed as though they were to carry away with them into oblivion all that was black and sinister in their way of living, and would leave behind them only their brave tradition of simple courage, of steadfast hearts and love for a wild, free life, a tradition that would touch the valley with magic and romance for all time.

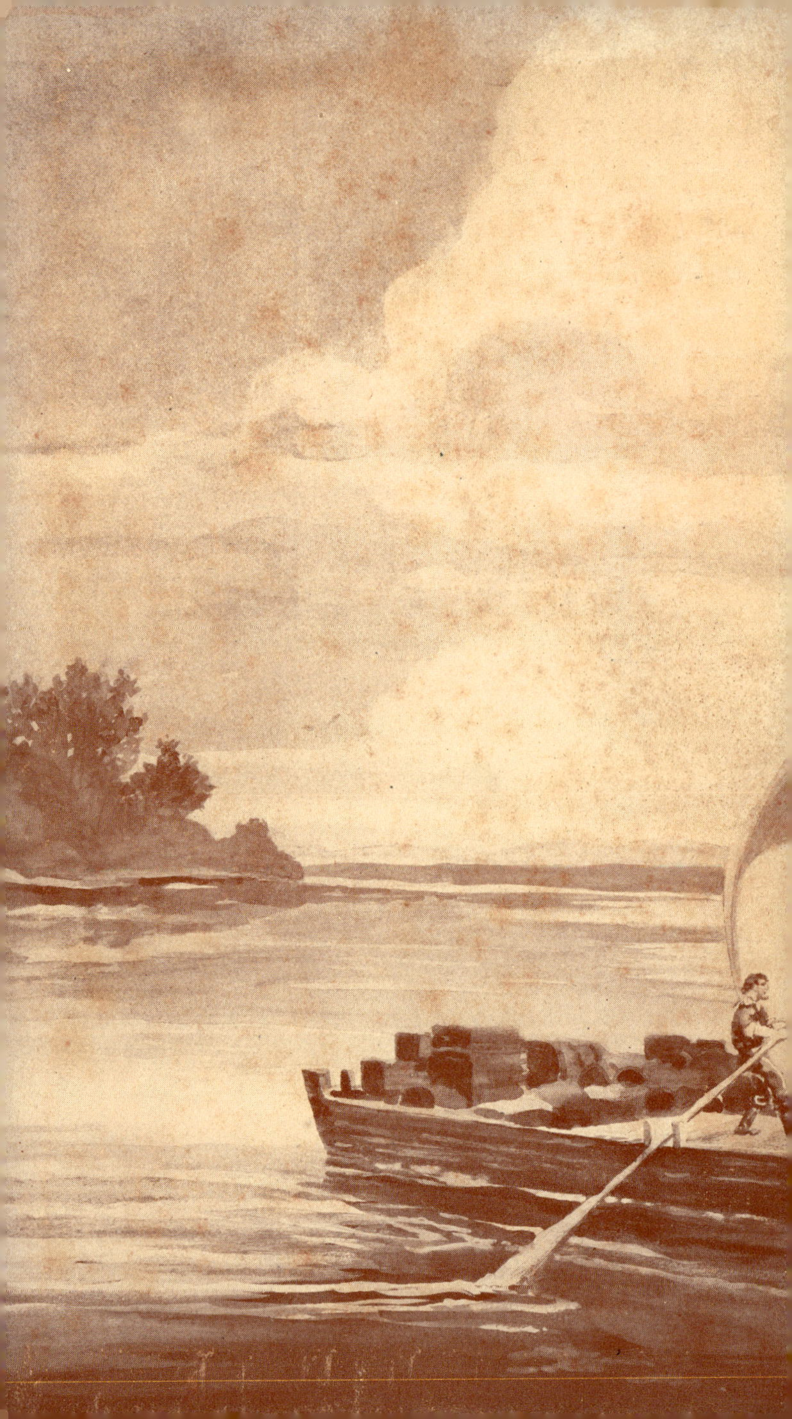